The

*Languages*

of

*Love*

Christine Brooke-Rose

Forthcoming reprint titles:

*A Grammar of Metaphor*
*The Sycamore Tree*
*Dear Deceit*
*The Middlemen*
*Go When You See The Green Man Walking*

*by* Christine Brooke-Rose

Forthcoming titles:

*The Letters of Christine Brooke-Rose*
*Poems & Other Paraphernalia*

edited *by* G. N. Forester & M. J. Nicholls

*The Logαλφαgeis of kLeub^h: /lɑːf/; /lʌv/*

*by* Chretine Broke-Prose

other Verbivoracious titles @

www.verbivoraciouspress.org

# The

## *Languages*

## of

## *Love*

# Christine Brooke-Rose

◧

Verbivoracious Press

Glentrees, 13 Mt Sinai Lane, Singapore

This edition published in Great Britain & Singapore

by Verbivoracious Press

www.verbivoraciouspress.org

Copyright © 2014 Verbivoracious Press

Text Copyright © 2014 The Estate of Christine Brooke-Rose

All rights reserved. No part of this publication may be re-produced, stored in an electronic or otherwise retrieval system, or transmitted in any form or by any means, electronic, mechanical, digital imaging, re-cording, otherwise, without the prior consent of the publisher.

The Estate has asserted the moral right of Christine Brooke-Rose to be identified as the author of this work.

ISBN: **978-981-07-9375-3**

Printed and bound in Great Britain & Singapore

First published in Great Britain by Secker & Warburg 1957.

## *Chapter One*

"BUT don't you think, Miss Grampion," said the professor beyond the long, wide table, "that palatal diphthongisation in fourteenth century Kentish may have been optional?"

His polite tone was smothered in gravel, as if it could only have come from the other side of the grave. Julia was conscious of nothing save his vast bulk and hairiness—shaggy, whitening blond hair clouding around a matching moon-face and curdling down in side whiskers to a startling handlebar moustache. He looked like Grendel's mother, bleached by many seas. And this was the final battle, in slow-motion, as if underwater.

Julia twirled a forelock nervously around her finger as she looked at the passage in front of her.

"Well, yes," she replied, slowly. The question made no sense at all. She briefly glimpsed a mediaeval bureaucrat, rather like Chaucer's Sergeant of the Lawe who "semed bisier than he was", issuing a proclamation: 'From 23:59 on the 16$^{th}$ April 1340, diphthongisation will be optional in the County of Kent.' She blinked away whimsy and strained to poise her voice.

"Surely, sir, the problem is really whether the diphthongs were rising or falling?" The "sir" habit was a relic from the Air Force. "I mean, that is what affects the metre, and, in this case, my interpretation." She took confidence from this and added, pompously, "I am only concerned with the poetry."

Dr Reeves looked up from the other end of that interminable table. "Yes, of course. A very fresh approach. But you are dealing with a dead language, you know." He had a plump, handsome face, and he was younger than the others. But just as Nordic. Philologists always seemed to be Nordic, seeking their Old Norse souls in lost sounds and syllables. Her supervisor sat between them, pink and bald and taciturn.

It went on and on. Grendel's mother was nothing if not meticulous. He had a sheaf of notes and went through them point by point, monopolising the examination. She wondered with dread whether Dr Reeves would have as many queries. But if he had, the professor hardly gave him a chance to produce them. It seemed unfair that he should have all his notes in front of him and she only her thesis. He could throw obscure citations from other texts at her, texts of which she suddenly felt she had never even heard, while she could only stick obstinately to the evidence she had provided.

"On page 327," and she turned it up hurriedly, gazing blankly at the strangely familiar typescript as if it were a tenth century fragment of a forgotten epic, copied by a neurotic scribe, "your footnote refers to Dan Michel," the professor said. "What do you think of his preterite forms, in this particular instance?"

"Well, these are irregular. I mean, from an Old Kentish point of view."

An idiotic phrase. At the other end of the table, Dr Reeves smiled to himself. She saw an Old Kentishman peering out of the ninth century at the preterite forms used by Dan Michel in the fourteenth, shaking his head and muttering, "most irregular." In her attempt to adapt herself, Julia was slipping into the crazy jargon of the grammarians.

At last it was over. She was, presumably and by the skin of her teeth, a Doctor of Philosophy, which covered a multitude of philological sins.

"Come and have a drink." Dr Reeves strolled down the corridor in a duffel coat, just as she emerged, washed and newly made up, from the cloakroom. "You must be feeling dazed. Two full hours of it."

"I knew they'd try and trip me up on philology." She was only half aware, in her relief, that she had excluded him from the examiners' triumvirate. He had been the kindest, taking over, when he could, the defending role that should have been assumed by her supervisor. She looked at him gratefully. Perhaps his own doctorate was recently acquired and with as much pain. But no; he must have sailed through with flying colours. She had looked up his thesis, indeed, she had looked up all the works of her examiners as soon as she knew their names, in order to know, even if too late, just on how many academic toes she had trodden.

"You did very well. We're paid to be fierce, you know." He gently reasserted his examiner's identity, and then abruptly dropped it on going through the swing doors, as if he had left his gown at the hall-desk. To her surprise he walked towards the cars parked in the drive. To her further surprise he stopped in front of a pale green Lambretta and fixed his briefcase into the curved front.

"Do you mind riding on the back of this? I have to go on to Piccadilly afterwards and don't want to come back for it." She smiled and sat gingerly, side-saddle on the back-seat, hugging her thesis and her handbag. "Better keep one hand free to hold on. Here, I'll put the great work in front."

The Lambretta gave a heave and sprang forward smoothly. They emerged into the Tottenham Court Road, were caught in a traffic jam, and turned deftly into a small side-street. He pulled up outside a wine-bar and handed her back her thesis.

"What do you want with a PhD anyway? You're not the academic type—just look at them. You should be writing detective stories."

The compliment, if it were one, was ambiguous. Flustered, Julia decided to decode it as "you're much too attractive to fade away into an academic woman" and not as "your thesis just won't do".

"Do I look like a female novelist? I thought they were all battle-axes." She went down the steps at an angle to him, then, afraid of getting no response, added in what she tried to make a hard, experienced tone, "whatever career women take up, they have so much more against them than men. They're bound to look like battle-axes by the time they get there."

"Oh, come off it. Women novelists seem to start at eighteen nowadays."

It occurred to her that he was hardly the academic type himself. For several years she had slowly trained herself to avoid arrogant exclamations like "come off it" or "what utter nonsense", replacing these with "might you not be mistaken" and "you may be right, but I would suggest". He was brash and blasé, and she half expected him to say that with a little sleeping around any attractive girl could have a novel published.

But he didn't. He took her arm and led her towards the bar. The place was full of grey-suited grey-haired men, probably from the publishing houses clustered in the district, or learned Assistant Keepers from the British Museum. Bloomsbury contained so much more than the student world and she felt a little lost.

"I should think you need more than wine after that ordeal. Two dry sherries, please."

Julia went and sat down, stunned but oddly grateful that anyone, almost a stranger, should make any decision for her. Perhaps he would offer her an assistant lectureship.

He came towards her, bulky in his duffel coat, managing two glasses in one hand and his briefcase—now presumably empty of his report on her work—in the other. "Let's drink to Dr Grampion," he said, sitting down. "No, you can't drink to yourself. Here's to Middle Kentish diphthongs, rising, falling, down the hatch."

The generous helping of sherry certainly helped to diphthongise her anxious, empty stomach. She took three olives from the small plate on the table. "What am I going to do?" she spoke intensely, which was difficult with olives in her mouth.

He looked at her carefully for the briefest of seconds, then said casually, "have a solid lunch, I should think. Do you smoke?" he displayed a large gold and green leather cigarette-case.

"No, I mean, yes, thank you. I meant, about my career." She heard her voice sound solemn as the drink mellowed her and she unwittingly put on a lost little girl look, at once seeming to cast him in a new role. Through her now bewildered eyes she saw, not the examiner, kinder and better-looking than the others though still severe, nor the jocular man of the world he had seemed on the way, but a gentle, fatherly mentor, friend and guide, who would offer to take her under his dove-like scholastic wing. As he bent forward to light her cigarette, she noticed that the flesh under his chin was a little flabby, that his brow was heavily lined and his blue eyes underlined, and that some white hair mingled almost imperceptibly with the fair. He was miraculously wise, safe, and attractive.

"I mean, I only just scraped through that. I know I'm not really good enough to be an academic." She paused for contradiction. "I'm too erratic," she added brightly, relieved to have found an adjective that made her incompetence seem more interesting, after a little too much hopeful humility.

"There's plenty of work to be done in your field," he said, slowly. "If you'd like to come and see me in my college, I can suggest several articles—"

"Paid?"

"Good God, no. We're not literary journalists."

"But I have to earn a living. It's April now and my grants stops in June."

Without asking her, he took their glasses to the counter and came back with refills, after a chat with the barman. "Ours is an overcrowded profession." He sat down, laughing. "Too many brilliant products of the Welfare State."

"I'm a product of the Welfare State, in a way. But not brilliant," she added, both as a preventative and as an inducement.

"Really? You don't seem to be."

She assumed that he was ignoring the second part of their statement. "I mean, I haven't worked my way up through brilliance from a humble origin, which is the fashionable thing to have done these days."

"What nonsense. This is the fifties, not the thirties. Have another cigarette."

Julia shook her head and twirled her hair again, this time behind the ear. This man disorientated her. Too self-assured and up-to-date for an academic, he nevertheless was not a wit. And the examiner's manner emerged readily with any shop-talk.

"My education was a reward for services rendered. Quite undeserved—just a year in the Air Force after the war was over. Occupying Germany. I've bluffed my way through all along."

This time it worked.

"Oh, come, you've a very fine brain and a lively critical approach." He had said something like that during the *viva* and she had been reminded of a refugee acquaintance who wrote popular books called *Dostoievski—A New Approach, Dostoievski and Emerson—An Approach*. "The trouble is," Dr Reeves went on, "one can't be a mediaevalist without being a philologist." She felt suitably crushed. He was talking with his cigarette, now half-smoked, in his mouth, and she watched irritably as it jogged up and down with each word, like a shuttle. "But I know how you feel. People like you and me don't really fit in." She rose again to the flattery of this unexpected bracketing. "I'm only tolerated as an eccentric. I'm mainly interested in rather off-beat literary aspects, as you know." She didn't. The thesis and articles she had looked up were crammed with erudite discussion of dialect forms and manuscript problems. She said so.

"That's what I mean," he replied. "One has to be able to do it." As an academic brush-off, it was gentle enough. But she suddenly felt tired, hungry, full of sherry and self-pity. He looked at her crestfallen face and smiled. "You're tired." He echoed her mood. "I should take a holiday."

"Can't afford it."

"Haven't you got a home you could go to? What about your parents?"

"Julia looked into her glass. She hated this question, which always led to an apology. "My father was killed in Africa. My mother in the Blitz."

"I'm very sorry."

She gave him an embarrassed half-smile and brusquely reverted to philology. "What on earth does it matter how *ea* was pronounced in fourteenth century Kentish, anyway?"

"In itself, perhaps it doesn't. But one can hardly discuss the literary merits of a poem without being able to place it and date it, and emend it where the manuscript is doubtful."

She was annoyed. "Of course I can do it, but it just doesn't interest me. There are enough people fascinated by the bare bones of language to do that work, and I prefer to work from edited texts. Besides," she went on aggressively, "this kind of pure phonology is hopelessly old-fashioned. You're all completely out of touch with what's going on in modern linguistics. In the Department of Afro-Asian Philology they have quite different methods. You can't apply the old concepts of sound and grammar to those languages. It's a science there, with machines." She thought of Paul with his tonometer and felt very clever.

"I know," he said, quietly, "but machines are no use on dead men." He glanced at her, aware of his tactlessness, and added, laughing, "unless a spiritualist recalled the scribe of the Beowulf manuscript, and even then a machine wouldn't be much use. It would be simpler just to ask him why he introduced all those Northern elements when he so obviously came from the South West."

She smiled wanly. "You know," she confided in a rather drunken way, "I don't *believe* in palatalisation."

He looked amused. "It's hardly a matter for belief, my dear. It happened, at certain stages in our language. It affected the way people pronounced things in different parts of the country. It affected the way poets rhymed words and balanced their sounds. There's no basic difference between that and finding out how a live African speaks. The bare bones of language, as you call them, are our only means of communication, both with each other and with the past. Aren't you interested in nuances?"

Julia sensed a flaw in his argument, but her own capacity for logic had turned into a sponge. "You rarely get anything as subtle as nuance from historical phonetics," she insisted. "Of course it's amusing to know that Chaucer is taking off the Northern dialect in one of his tales, but the difference is dead, to us. A snob joke is only funny if the norm is so natural to you that you're unconscious it is the norm. Like BBC English and Lancashire comedians. And even today it isn't all that funny."

"I wasn't talking about snob humour." He seemed to spark off from the friction of her resentment. "I meant the glimpses of life one sees from the very sound-changes themselves."

"Don't! They nearly drove me mad. I dream of sound-changes." She gulped down her sherry and waved away the memories. "I still wake up working out every stage by which *odium* becomes *annoy*, or how *cognitum* becomes *quaint*. But I find the change of meaning much more interesting." She leant forward confidently. "It has changed and not changed: hatred is after all most annoying and cognisance is a very quaint affair."

Dr Reeves looked at her with renewed interest mingled with delight. "And yet"—he waved a mock-reproving finger at her—"if you didn't know from phonology that they were the same words, you wouldn't know the semantic development, would you? But even a pure sound change can bring something of the past to life. Think of the Old French word *escarn*, rushing in ahead to catch the Southern English change from *o* to *a*. It's the only Norman word to do so. *Scorn*." His voice was rich and deep as he said the word. "Why should *scorn* be borrowed so much earlier than other

Norman words with *a*? It throws a fascinating light on occupational psychology, don't you think?"

Julia hadn't looked at it that way, feeling vaguely that there was something rather Walter-Scottish about his attitude to philology, which was oh, such a dry and serious subject. Yet she herself had turned a pretty quip of etymology. She suddenly felt very stupid.

"Why did I take all this up," she dramatised, "when all I can do now is to go back to my garret and starve while I write novels, as you said? The sort that are wrapped in garish jackets: breast-sellers."

He laughed. "Do you really live in a garret? Where?"

"Well, it's a top-floor room in Gower Street."

"What number?"

She told him.

"I'll call around one day and see how the fifty-seventh chapter is going. And now I'm afraid I must fly. I'm meeting my wife for lunch and I'm late already."

They came out into the street. She thanked him, lamely.

He took her hand and held it in both of his, just a little too long, saying, "good luck. And don't despair. I should take a long rest. Your brain will feel like a vegetable after all that strain. But things turn up, you'd be surprised."

He climbed onto his Lambretta and scootered off towards Oxford Street. She jay-walked through the traffic-jam of St Giles, vaguely hoping to be run over, and lunched alone in the cafeteria, deep in the noisy bowels of Lyons Corner House.

## Chapter Two

PAUL BRODRICK smiled at the tall, willowy African who stood shyly just inside the door of his small room in the Department of Afro-Asian Philology. But for his European clothes he might have stepped straight out of King Solomon's Mines, he was so very tall. His receding hair was shaped in two triangular tufts jutting from either side of a high, shining brow, looking like a dark felted tricorn, curiously tilted back. Soft brown eyes gazed wisely from deep sockets, and a double hollow emphasised the cheek-bone, one below it in front, one at the side.

"Come in, Hussein," said Paul. "Sit down. I've worked out the lists. I want you to help me with these inflections. They seem to be just aspirated, as if you simply stopped breathing for the genitive."

Hussein flashed a wide white grin as he sat down on the other side of the desk, which was covered with large sheets of statistics, graphs and lists of sound-occurrences. "Like the flick of a whip on a horse's back."

Paul laughed. "That is not an accurate description of the sound, you know."

Hussein looked hurt. Then he smiled triumphantly. "Like the lion hitting the grass of the prairie with his tail."

He spoke English extremely well. Only certain consonant groups with *r* gave him trouble. He watched Paul concentrating on his lists. "No po-et-tery to-day?" he asked.

"No poetry, Hussein, just words." To him these were two separate concepts.

"Songs are in hundreds," said Hussein, "like the waves in the sea. The man who is not full of them, his bowels are cut out."

Paul smiled.

"I'm sorry. I must get these done for Professor Kriss. I promised them for yesterday. We can translate some more poems tomorrow." He looked at his notes again. Hussein sighed and settled down.

"Let's take the word *dog*. How do you say in Sanuri, *the dog walks*?"
Hussein said it.
"Now leave out *walks*, but say *the dog* as if you were going to say *walks*."
He had switched on a recording machine, but also listened carefully for the inflection and wrote down a phonetic sign.
"How do you say *the nose of the dog*?"
Hussein said it, and repeated it without *the nose*.
"And how do you say, *come on, dog*?"
Hussein flashed another wide white grin and whistled, as if calling a dog. Then he subsided into a paroxysm of deep tropical laughter. Paul looked up with a pained expression. But tropical laughter, like African tick-fever, is infectious, and soon they were both helplessly producing volleys of unphilological sounds that would have alarmed a tonometer to bursting point, like two hyenas with a Hottentot click.
At this moment Angel Kriss came in. Professor Angela Kriss. Her cropped white hair went grey with shock, suddenly matching her face and clothes. She removed a pair of thick-rimmed glasses and said acidly:
"Is one permitted to share in the hilarity?"
Paul had to make a swift choice between the lameness of repeating an evanescent joke and the rudeness of refusing to share it. He decided for the latter.
"Oh, good morning, Professor. It was just a little—er—Moslem mirth." He knew that if he said "phonetic fun" she would insist on hearing it, and then be unamused. But Moslem mirth was calculated, at some risk, to side-track her into Anglican dignity. Her attitude to African studies was distinctly unanthropological. "And what can I do for you, Professor Kriss?"
"Well when you have finished apostatising with Allah, I would like to see the lists of muted-vowel vibrations you were preparing for me. If they are ready," she added pointedly.
"I'm working on them now," said Paul, and felt mortified. Angela Kriss always mortified him, by making him feel inefficient and vague. Left to himself, he could be the dryest paragon of statistical precision; confronted with her, he was a poet and playboy among scientists, a shooting star in a mathematical universe, thousands of light years away.

"I'll let you have them as soon as possible. Tomorrow, or perhaps the next—"

"Tomorrow, by ten o'clock." Excluded from mirth, she obtruded rank. "I wanted to collate them today, you know. Well, I'll expect you then. Good-bye, Mr Abdillahi, nice to have seen you." She hardly looked at Hussein, who had risen politely when she entered. If he had been offended by her casual reference to Allah, he had shown no sign of it, but he winced now at the appellation. Nevertheless he opened the door for her.

"Prosper," he said, bowing as she marched out.

"Why does she call me always with my father's name?" he asked Paul as he walked back to the desk.

"Well, she's interested mainly in your language, not in your customs. She feels she doesn't know you well enough to call you by your Christian name, as I do."

"But I am not a Christian."

"I mean your first name. Mr Hussein Abdillahi is too long for her."

"It is strange, her hair is white like the leaves of the harri-tree."

"Why shouldn't it be?"

"She should like long words."

Paul laughed. "She does, if they're down on a list, or coming out of a machine. She doesn't like having to say them herself."

Hussein was reminded of work. "Shall I tell you some poems now?"

Resentment of Angela Kriss mingled with a much deeper affection for Hussein in Paul's surrender. And Sanuri poetry, with its weird imagery and hypnotic assonances, roused a different man in him, a man he suddenly needed to be, if only for a while. Besides, he could listen to muted-vowel assonances in a long poem of tender passion as well as in short cold sentences. Couldn't he?


At four o'clock, Paul took Hussein down to the Common Room, where an obligatory tea-party was being held before a lecture on new methods in linguistics, by a visiting professor of Comparative Philology from Helsinki, to whom he was introduced.

"This is my assistant, Mr Hussein Abdillahi, from Sanuri, in East

Africa."

"Ah, yes. Enchanted," said Professor Nieminen. He contrasted oddly with Hussein, being nearly as tall, but much broader in the shoulders and completely bald "You are working on Sanuri, yes?"

"Sanuri and Isharood. Hussein is most useful, he knows both. A rare case of bilingualism. His mother was Isharood."

"Ah, yes. Enchanting," said Professor Nieminen. "I hope the languages belong to the same group? We always say in Finland—we joke of course—that it is a grave sin for an agglutinating man to marry a non-agglutinating woman." He did not have to laugh at his joke, because he wore a permanent, wry, Finno-Ugrian smile which could have served all levels of humour and high seriousness for numerous civilisations. "But the religions, they are the same?"

"Most Isharood are Nestorians, some are Catholic, and some are Moslem, like the Sanuris."

The professor turned to Hussein. "And you are a Moslem, yes, Mr—er?"

Hussein assented.

"You do not mind working with us Christians?"

"Mister Borrodick is Catholic," Hussein replied as if this explained all.

"That is good."

'Is it?' wondered Paul, and thought of Julia.

"But he has only one angel on his shoulder," Hussein went on, "it is very sad. We have two angels." He crossed his arms to touch each of his angels. "One writes down all the sins, and all the good actions also, the other is the Guardian Angel."

"Does the Recording Angel write it down when you are sorry you've sinned?" asked Paul.

"Yes, if I am sorry before eight hours, he crosses it out."

"That's too easy."

"The tail and repentance go behind," Hussein announced solemnly, and then added, with a dazzle of teeth and wicked eye: "Some sins, I am not sorry for them before eight hours. I want to continue."

'Julia, Julia, Julia,' thought Paul, but he laughed.

Professor Nieminen's smile did not shift a millimetre, and a Lutheran soul seemed to peer for a moment with mild distaste from unangelic grey eyes. "And what is the documentation?" he asked Hussein, who looked puzzled. Nieminen turned to Paul. "How old is the first Sanuri manuscript?"

"Oh, about 1949, I wrote it down myself."

The Finno-Ugrian smile remained intact. "Have you yourself been to Sanuri, Dr Brodrick?"

"I was there for three years. Hussein was assigned to me by the government to help me, and I brought him back. Can't do without him, but unfortunately he's due to return soon."

"Ah, yes. Enchanting. And will he take you with him this time?"

"Well, I shall be going back for another year, but I'm not sure when."

"What do you do in Sanuri, Mr—er?" The professor turned to Hussein.

"I was a teacher. Now I will organise Birrtish pogroms."

Nieminen looked even more lost than among the angels.

"Educational programmes," Paul explained. "So far their school teaching has consisted almost entirely of epics and love-poems, with occasional breaks for arithmetic. Hussein wants to introduce a little variety. Such as English epics and love-poems."

"There is a language in the Caucasus," the professor announced, "which has forty-five cases. How many do you have, Mr—er?"

The answer, "five or seven, according to your point of view," came from Angela Kriss, who had a finely developed sense of dramatic entrances, if not of *bienséance*.

"I'm giving a little party for Professor Nieminen tonight, at my flat," she said. "Will you come, Dr Brodrick, with your fiancée, of course. And you, Mr Abdillahi."

"Thank you very much, Miss Kriss." Hussein bowed.

"But I was going to work on those case-endings this evening," said Paul guiltily, "I don't think—"

"Drop 'em," she interrupted, swinging her empty teacup with an equally empty rhetorical gesture. "My dear boy, you worry too much, far too conscientious, no hurry at all. Do your young men work so hard in Helsinki, Professor? Ah!" She took out a man's vast silver watch from the breast pocket of her grey suit, and turned to Paul and Hussein. "You'd better go in, it's time. I'm in the chair, so we'll wait a little. I'll expect you at nine."

Paul smiled and went dutifully into the adjoining room. Hussein seemed to shrink, miraculously, into the more average height of the desultory groups moving towards the lecture. Like a shade spattered and then extinguished by strong white light, he filtered through them and slipped quietly away.

## Chapter Three

*EL ANDALUZ*, in Soho, provided a rather unquiet *ambiente* in which to be dined and wined by one's publisher, but Bernard Reeves had suggested it, although he was the guest, because he loved the guitar. His Nordic temperament responded to Spanish popular music as a vegetable responds to the sun, and his literary personality, which he was wearing tonight, always seemed to drop off him like an unsewn coat, unless constantly seamed up again by the quick machinery of those strummed out rhythms. Some of the more traditional ballads, too, of the kind which started with *Pongan atención señores*, reminded him of mediaeval romances, reintegrating for a moment the more scattered fringes of his schizoid interests.

As yet the strumming merely purred faintly from the inner recesses of the restaurant. Bernard sat now in an imitation *patio* under an imitation palm-tree, sipping dry sherry and waiting for Justin Jacob, of Tweedie and Tweedie, to join him.

"My dear chap, so sorry I'm late. Got held up with the lawyers, going through a manuscript for obscene libel. Brilliant novel, the whole situation's becoming a farce. How are you?" Justin Jacob sat down, darkly congruous under the fake palm-tree. He ordered a manzanilla, smoothly, in Spanish. "How are the proofs?"

"Nearly finished. Hell of a job, checking all the facts. I've had to add a few notes." Justin looked alarmed. "You'll have the whole thing by the end of the month, I hope. It all looks incredibly tedious, not a Tweedie book at all."

"Well, we want to build up a scholarly and critical list. We've somehow acquired a smart reputation for highbrow pornography and labyrinthine symbolic novels translated from German."

Bernard felt uncomfortable. He rather liked *Götterdämmerung*, in any form.

"Have to balance it out a bit." Justin smiled with raised black eyebrows, exactly equipoising irony and sensitivity. But his idea of himself was always a few years behind the times: the finely sensuous young face had thickened, slightly but in direct ratio to the thinning of his hair.

"I have a proposition for you which might link both aspects of your list," said Bernard. "I got interested in it while doing the book on Courtly Love."

"Oh?" Justin's tone suggested a mild surprise that anyone, author, reader or lover, could still be interested in Courtly Love this season, even under the Tweedie imprint.

"How about a symposium on the treatment of adultery in literature—all over the world, I mean, with contributions from classicists, Orientalists, mediaevalists, and so on?"

"*The Writer's Whore.*" Justin chuckled and got up. "Shall we go in?"

They walked into the restaurant, laughing. A burst of flamenco greeted them, as a high nasal tenor voice wailed on a tensely modulating larynx.

> *Por la noche ere' de roca*
> *Por el dia pan de fio-o-o-o'*
> *Me tienes aprisiona-a-a-a'o*
> *En lo' beso' de tu bo-o-o-oca*

"Well, it's not quite that," said Bernard as they sat down. "The loves and pleasure of married ladies rather."

"Free but complicated instead of priced and simple," Justin put in.

Bernard smiled tolerantly, intent on selling his idea without too much compromise. "What I'm interested in is the effect of social conventions on literary presentation."

"Should tie up with all the bother about libel laws, obscene or otherwise. Would you be general editor?"

"That's the idea. I'd thoroughly enjoy learning all about the subject in other literatures."

"So would I."

"There are lots of chaps I can rope in, for Sanskrit, Chinese—"

"Won't it get rather out of hand?"

"Adultery usually does."

> *Porque no vale la pen-e-ena*

# The Languages of Love: Chapter Three

They ordered *paella* and wine.

"Of course, I'll have to be careful about the tone. I don't want to get chucked out of my job. At least, I wouldn't mind, but I can't afford it."

"Surely the safeguard lies in getting all those experts," said Justin. "I'm certain that experts are always delighted with any research which involves erotic motifs. At the same time, the university would hardly want to lose the lot."

"Blackmail!" But Bernard was pleased with Justin's easy response. "It will be strictly a scholarly affair, all the same, though quotations would have to be translated, naturally."

They talked on, silenced only by the castanets and the stamping when four buxom girls in flares of red and white frill danced a *Sevillana*, their white arms a little too plump for the snakes effect, their heads not quite arrogantly tossing too little pride on which to trample with a swift rattle of heels.

"This isn't the real goods," Justin scoffed. "Have you seen the *gitanas* dance? These girls are Spanish town-tarts."

Bernard's rapture was creased. "Well, only in the theatre." He had never been to Spain, but as a scholar he disliked being taken in by the fake. "I have to go to a party after this," he said, to change the subject. "Angela Kriss, do you know her?"

"Should I?" Justin mentally searched other publishers' lists, but drew a blank.

"No. My milieu rather than yours. Philologist, but unusually human. Quite mad. The party's apparently in honour of some formidable Finn. Why don't you come along?"

*Tengo una casita cerca del Guadalquivir*, a female voice intoned desperately, to the cruelly tender plucking of gut-strings, heart-strings, and vocal chords.


Through the mosaic of heads, bald, grey, sandy and brown, Bernard saw Julia come in long before she noticed him. She was accompanied by a remarkably tall African and a dark young man with wide, staring blue eyes and a thin rim of beard which made him look like a Rouault portrait, edged in black. He was only half a head shorter than the African. It was an unusual escort for a budding philologist.

She was not beautiful. For one thing, her hair was khaki. Short, curling thickly and well-groomed, but khaki, which made her green eyes look field-grey and at war. They were too wide apart and her face was too round. She had slim shapely legs, but her figure was just a little too full. She wore a low cut black dress of some clinging woollen material. No, she was not beautiful, but Bernard couldn't take his eyes off her.

"Bernard, dear, you must come and meet Pekka," boomed Angela Kriss, "he's an absolute charmer. Why didn't you come to his lecture? I sent you an invitation. It was tremendous fun. Phonemes, you know." She marched him up to Professor Nieminen. "Pekka, this is Dr Bernard Reeves, he's a great admirer of yours." Bernard was left, cluelessly polite, with the formidable Finn.

Angela Kriss was wearing the same nondescript grey coat and skirt, but her social manner contrasted violently with the dry, restrained scientific precision she bestowed on muted vowel vibrations. She talked entirely in superlatives, having acquired her conversational style in the twenties and stuck to it. The rest of her mind was morphological and machine-made. She was thus contrary in the extreme and alarmingly direct.

"Who are you?" she said to Justin Jacob, "is there anyone you want to meet?"

"I take it you are my hostess," he replied, and introduced himself. "Who is the gorgeous Negro prince?" I'd like to meet him."

"And so you shall, m'dear. He's one of my assistants, Mr Abdillahi. *The most* enormously charming and intelligent man to come out of darkest Africa. He's teaching Sanuri without tears."

They moved up towards the trio, who were deep in conversation. Justin was introduced, in extravagant terms, and Angel Kriss stalked off to disconcert her other guests.

"Mister Jacob?" Hussein grinned happily. "You have an angel, with a ladder, on your shoulder?"

Justin looked bewildered for a moment, then laughed.

"My angel has long climbed back to heaven in despair," he said with a lewd smile, "and left me to sleep on my stone pillow." He looked Hussein in the eyes and narrowed his own, then raised his eyebrows very slightly, edging closer. Hussein beamed at him innocently. "But you haven't got a drink. Let me get you something—my dear," he clarified with a more hopelessly European attempt to cross the barriers of race, continents, and cultures.

"No, thank you very much. We do not drink the hydromel," Hussein replied with a disarming flash of teeth that bit Justin in the guts. "I stand and see you."

Justin Jacob was flustered by this last remark. Was it a different kind of code? He edged even closer, so that the hand holding his glass touched the lapel of Hussein's jacket. "Well, tell me all about yourself. I like you."

Hussein beamed again.

"I too," he said ambiguously.

"Hello, Justin, how're you doing?" Bernard had at last disentangled himself from the philological tentacles of the formidable Finn.

"Fine, just fine," Justin grumbled, furious at the interruption. "This is Hussein. My friend Bernard."

Bernard grasped the situation and gladly took the hint, his eye on Julia. "Well, I won't butt in, you seem to be deep in conversation. Hello," he tapped her on the shoulder. "I see you've recovered from this morning's exertions."

As in the wine-bar, he avoided a formal "Miss Grampion", calling her nothing. English was usefully imprecise in its social gradations.

She turned, surprised. "Dr Reeves!" she exclaimed, more honestly. But her face lit up. He noticed the sudden fissure on either side of her mouth when she smiled. He noticed her mouth, too; full and distinctly carved. She wore a very slender gold crucifix, with a chain so fine it was hardly visible on her pale olive skin.

"I didn't recognise you at first," he lied, "you look taller in high heels. And that dress!" His eye wandered.

"Paul, this is Dr Reeves, one of my examiners. The kindest." She laughed delightedly. "Paul Brodrick. My fiancé," she added after a moment's hesitation. "This *is* a philological party, isn't it? A fling of phoneticians."

"I know. I got stuck with the guest of honour. He was going on about the survival of the dual. So much more precise than the plural, for two people. He said there was one in I forget what language, which tells you how far apart they have to stand." He was standing very close.

She edged away slightly, but her eyes twinkled. "Very useful at parties, I should think?"

Paul smiled at her. "Touché, Dr Reeves?"

He laughed. "Unfortunately not." Bernard turned to her, making up his mind suddenly. "You wouldn't like to come in on a book I may be editing? No money in it, I'm afraid, till it's ready, and then not very much, probably." Paul moved off tactfully. "But it should be rather fun, and the sort of thing you could do in your spare time."

"Philology."

"No, adultery."

She was visibly shaken. He explained, kindly, apologetically. "I was going to do the mediaeval contribution myself, at least the French and English. But as editor, I think I should keep off. Do you read Old French?"

"Yes, but—"

"The treatment of the theme in the early English romances is fascinating," he went on, "it's already so puritan. Just look at Sir Gawain's incredibly dim behaviour with the Green Knight's wife."

"Well, there's a theory he was a vegetable myth," said Julia, "so what do you expect? In this climate." She adapted herself easily, too easily but superficially, to what she thought people were like, catching the sparks of flippancy as quickly as she would a smouldering mood of introspection or the flaring of passion. She had often caught herself colouring her vowels differently when talking to lorry-drivers in her hitch-hiking days. "All the same," she added more seriously, "I'm astonished that you should be writing this sort of book."

"Oh, but it'll be very scholarly, not a—what did you call it—breastseller. And not a vulgarisation, or I wouldn't ask you—"

"Do you want a general mediaeval contributor or several specialists?" she asked. "I mean, I only know a little Italian, and no Spanish. And there's all the Middle High German stuff." Her enthusiasm was as sudden as it was impractical.

He longed to suggest taking her out of that *mêlée* of maniacs, discussing it over a drink, seeing her home. But he knew better than to press his advantage too soon.

"Well, it's all very much in the air as yet," he replied. "I only proposed it to my publisher this evening. He's here, actually, you must meet him."

In fact, Julia didn't meet him. Bernard drifted away, retaining the initiative with an "I'll get in touch with you." He left, soon after, with a somewhat snuffed out Justin Jacob. She was stranded with the philological Finn.

"Of course," he was saying, "there was no future in the Indo-European period."

"And yet," she replied, refusing to be serious, "here we are."

## Chapter Four

JULIA peered sleepily out of her front door into a May morning, which was bleakly drizzling its monthlessness down the hypnotism of dark brick and railings that called itself Gower Street. She was still in her dressing gown, although students were hurrying into the Drama School. She quickly snatched her half-pint of milk and crept in again, smoothing down her hair. Two newspapers and three letters for her lay on the hall table. One was only printed matter, and one an unsealed invitation. She puzzled for a while over the handwriting of the third, which was stamped WC1, then she stumbled upstairs. Impetuous in big things, Julia liked to keep small pleasures for the right moment, and the opening of mail was one of them: it had to be done over coffee.

She was resting. For a fortnight she had done nothing at all. Her days consisted of getting up late, writing a few letters, lunching with Paul, catching up on her mending, making a new dress, rearranging her books, having supper with Paul. She had thought that at last she would read all the books she wanted to read, but she couldn't even open one. She had sunk to crossword puzzles, and was becoming empathic with the mind of the man on the *Daily Chronicle*.

Her room was fairly large but in some disorder. Underclothes were thrown over an armchair, shoes had been kicked off near the grate. A blue whipcord dress hung from the half-open door of the wardrobe and the desk by the window was covered with shambles of newspapers, sewing materials, and curious shapes of green poplin tacked together or loosely pinned on thin patterns: she liked wearing black, with here and there a touch of bright colour, or alternatively plain bright colours, with here and there a touch of black. An open cocoa-tin stood by the gas ring in the corner by the desk, and one unwashed cup; but other crockery was neatly stacked on the shelves below. The bed, behind the door, was unmade, and its pillow thrown out on the nearest armchair.

## The Languages of Love: Chapter Four

Julia put the coffee on and toasted some bread while she looked up her stars in the morning paper: *a lowering of tone in emotional prospects*, they announced. She glanced down the back of the other paper, which was a weekly, and saw that Cairo University was inviting applications for the post of either assistant professor or lecturer in Reinforced Concrete. She sighed, laid the table carefully and sat down at last to have her breakfast and open her letters, in order of unimportance. The printed matter was a circular from the Mediaeval Society, which she tossed towards the waste paper basket, missing it. The second envelope contained an invitation from Georgina Raymond to a party the following week. Presumably with Paul. The third—she looked down the small, spidery handwriting and started twirling her hairs as she tried to guess: male, very large, pedantic, yet generous. But this evoked no picture. Then she gave a small gasp of surprise, mingled with fear. It was from her examiner, Grendel's mother.

*Dear Miss Grampion*, she read.

*I wonder if you would be interested in applying for an assistant lectureship which is becoming vacant in my department. Mr Drummond, who has it now, is leaving us for Edinburgh. It would mainly involve taking students through Old and Middle English set texts, with the usual commentaries on manuscript problems, etc. I am not of course in a position to offer you the job, as the Board will have to consider all applications, but I was most impressed with your thesis and would strongly support your application.*

*Perhaps you would like to come to dinner with us one evening, when I could tell your more about it. Kindly telephone me at the above.*

*Yours Sincerely,*
*J. Jarvis-Anderson*

"So!" said Julia aloud to herself. "The most cruel was the most impressed, the kindest, least. How like them." She wasn't sure whether "them" meant examiners in particular, academics in general, or just men.

She lit a cigarette. With the first ten puffs she inhaled wild excitement. Her career was beginning. She was wanted, actually wanted, in an academic capacity. With the next twenty puffs she inhaled the delicious flattery of his words: *I was most impressed . . . would strongly support your application*. But as the cigarette drew to an end, she felt gradually much smaller and about to be stubbed. *I am not of course in a position . . .* And even so: *the usual commentaries on manuscript problems . . . set texts.* She saw herself go though the minutiae of scansion, dialect forms, emendation, haplography, *hapax legomena* and *anacolutha* in Beowulf. That wasn't what she wanted at all. She began to invent a whimsical love affair between Anna Coluthon, who was too inconsequential, and Hapax Legomenon, who was too unique.

There was a knock on the door, and in came the landlady, with bright blue hair, a square white face and a splodge of lipstick that matched the large flowers on the cotton overall which only just enveloped her ample figure. She looked like a *tricolore* planted in a poppy field.

"Oh, hello, Mrs Moffat. I'm afraid I'm not dressed yet, do you want to do the room?"

" 'sall right, dear, you take it easy, I'll do Miss Reeno first." Monique Renaud was a French student who had the room next door. "Your boyfriend phoned this morning at 'arf past eight."

"Paul? Oh, any message?"

"Well, by the time I was out of the—er, you know, and up the stairs, 'e'd rung orf."

"But how—"

"Oh, I knew it was 'im, from the way 'e rang."

For a moment Julia took this quite literally as perfectly possible. Then she laughed. But Mrs Moffat was entirely serious.

"D'you like me new candlesticks?" she asked proudly. "I got them for your taytatayts." They were made of bright green porcelain, with coloured berries. "I think they're ever so nice. Like futuristic shoes."

Before Julia could answer the telephone rang downstairs.

"That's 'im again. You'd better go down, luv, or 'e'll stop before the likes of me can get there. So impatient, these young men."

Julia flew down, credulous again. It might be for anyone in the house, but that ring was Paul's own. It was, too.

"Darling. Are you up?"

"Just about."

"Look, I'm taking the morning off. I must see you."

"Of course." This was unlike Paul. "Darling, anything wrong?"

There was a pause.

"I had a letter from Father Alston this morning."

She stood very still and said nothing.

"Can you meet me for coffee at *The Groves of Academe*, as soon as you can make it?"

"Twenty minutes."

"Fine."

"Bye. Darling," she added just as the line went dead.

She dressed in five, tidied up her room, make the bed, washed up the breakfast in ten, and on the dot entered the espresso-bar. Apart from the usual forestry, here representing *The Groves*, the café was designed for the pullulating modern dregs of the Bloomsbury Group. One wall was a set of false bookshelves, another was decorated entirely with examination papers; the tables were flat lecture desks; a large side-alcove was aimed at the drama students, with masques and stage photographs, and the owner was making a fortune on youth's desire to romanticise its actually drab daily existence. At this moment, however, between coffee-time and lunch, the place was almost empty. Paul was already there, gazing at an untouched cup of coffee thickly blanketed with froth.

"Another cappuccino," he called out as she sat down. He looked paler than usual and his blue eyes stared wildly under the dark brows. He took her hand.

"Darling, oh darling."

She stroked his wrist in silence. Then her hand went up to his face and she fingered it gently, as if to memorise it, the high cheek-bones, the decisive lips, the absurd edge of beard outlining his strong chin and jaw.

"I love you, Paul."

"I love you."

An existentialist-looking girl brought her coffee. Julia moved her hand down. She put two spoonfuls of brown sugar in the cup and stirred, without drinking.

"Show me the letter."

Paul took out his wallet and produced an envelope from it. She looked at the sheets of paper unfolded on the table.

"What an unpleasant handwriting."

"Darling, don't start on that. How can you tell, anyway, at a glance?"

She turned it upside down, then sideways, examining the spacing between lines, between letters, the length of the downward and upward strokes, the margin. She knew she was just putting off having to read it.

"Look, three different ways of crossing the ts. No, four. Three, four, five gs. And the way he breaks before each s, and after, too."

"There's no point in analysing his character, you know." Paul started to stir his own coffee, also without drinking it.

"I never did like him." She gazed at the word "Church" which was curiously split up.

"Darling Julia. I've always adored your lapses in logic, but anticlericalism is rather irrelevant here. Father Alston may be the most abominable man as a man—though I don't think so myself—but as a priest he's only mouthpiece."

"Yes. I know."

She started to read the letter. It became very technical. A noisy group of drama students came in, laughing, and went in the side-alcove. He put his arm around her while she read. She was curling her hair round and round her fingers nervously, and her hand trembled as she turned each page.

"The gist of all this is," she said slowly when she had finished, "that Westminster refuses even to consider a case brought by a non-Catholic, and that even if they did it wouldn't stand a chance."

"That's about it."

"And they say they want converts."

"Darling, don't be bitter." He removed his arm.

"What the hell do you expect? Why should I be made to pay now for past ignorance? I'd never even heard of the Church's attitude to divorce. It never occurred to me then that I would one day want to marry a Catholic."

"Darling, I know, I know. If only you'd told me in the beginning, I wouldn't have pursued—"

"If only, if only!" She turned on him passionately. "If only one didn't meet anyone, didn't fall in love, didn't live."

"I meant, one can always stop, at the beginning."

"Can one? Anyway we didn't."

"No. We didn't. You were everything, everything I wanted." He took her hand again and pressed it so hard it hurt.

"Made to your measurements but not to God's." She suddenly wanted to cry, and took a mouthful of coffee to drown the lump in her throat. "I could hardly tell you the day we got engaged," she went on slowly, "that I'd been married before. It would have been like, well, admitting a flaw in the goods when sealing the bargain." He winced. "In any case, this kind of objection never even crossed my mind. Oh, darling," she put her other hand on his, which was still on her wrist, "I loved you. I only wanted to make sure of you."

"You made sure of me all right."

"I told you soon enough. You could have withdrawn then. But you didn't. You treated me like forbidden fruit, relishing it."

"You can be cruel, can't you?" Paul took his hand away to shade his eyes, which still gazed vacantly at the untouched coffee.

"I just can't understand the Church's attitude." She stared across the room at the sham rows of books that lined the wall opposite. "Here I am, willing to become a Catholic, accepting the whole bang lot. But they shut me out, because of a stupid mistake I made in my teens."

""They don't shut you out. You can still become a Catholic. But you can't remarry and remain one."

"That *is* shutting me out. Surely, of all people, they should allow one to repent and have a full Christian marriage?"

"Oh, darling, we've had all this out before. I can reel off all the answers if you want them. Your first marriage is the Christian one. You took vows in an Anglican church, to which you both belonged. But what's the point?"

"Oh, I know." A gaunt young man came in and sat down at the next table. He ordered a lemon tea and opened a large book. "It just seems so unfair. Neither of us believed in anything. How can it be a contract in the eyes of God, as they put it, if you don't believe in God at the time?" The young man looked up and then bent over his book, consciously assiduous. Julia glanced at the title: *Summa Theologica*.

"Look Paul," she went on in a low voice, "I haven't told you this, but after I left him, well, life in post-war Germany was pretty reckless, and I was jumping in and out of bed with almost anyone. If I've got anything to be ashamed of it's that, and not this ridiculous marriage. But that's precisely what doesn't count, it can all be washed out in the confessional." She fumbled in her bag for a cigarette.

"I think I'll have one, too, I need one." He normally didn't smoke till after lunch. She gave him one and lit it for him.

"What I did out of sheer innocence and kindness—or lack of moral courage to break it off—that's what's chalked up against me for ever and ever. It's absurd."

"Your attitude's so puritan." Paul spoke quietly. "Don't you see that shame has nothing to do with it? Your marriage wasn't a sin you've got to repent. A sacrament occurs whether you believe in it or not, whether your mind is on it or on the lady's hat in front."

"Even if I knew nothing about it." She put her head in her hand, singeing her hair with her cigarette.

"Careful, darling, don't burn yourself." He drew her hand gently away from her hair. "Please listen to me. There's no point in arguing about theological refinements. It won't change the Canon Law, or my position on it. I wanted to see you to suggest a compromise."

"You? Compromise?"

"I love you. You know that."

"Yes. I know that." Her voice trembled as she felt the tears surge up again. A stagey voice rose from the alcove: "Yes, but I object to *keeping my men*." Then it drowned in talk and laughter. The gaunt young man was making notes from Saint Thomas Aquinas, apparently oblivious of his surroundings.

"I want to marry you," said Paul very softly.

She stared at him.

"And abandon your faith?"

He flicked his cigarette carefully into the ashtray. "Faith isn't a thing you abandon. If you have it, you can't make a conscious choice not to have it, or you wouldn't have it."

"But you can lose it."

"Yes, you can lose it."

She looked into her coffee and said slowly, "I certainly wouldn't blame you."

"But I haven't lost it."

Julia gazed at him, troubled. She loved him then more than ever before. He had been ruffling his hair, which now fell on his forehead in an untidy brown fringe. She smoothed it back with her free hand. "Darling, what do you want?"

"There are ways. Lots of people are in the same situation, you know. The Church is kinder than you think, even though the law has to come down on one side of a hard case."

"And what do they do?"

"They can get married, for social propriety, in a civil court, and go to Mass, living together in continence."

Julia sat very still, watching her cigarette burn out. "Marriage to me, means children."

"To me, too."

"It's downright masochism."

"Or," said Paul, extinguishing his own cigarette rhythmically, "they can attend Mass, without taking the Sacrament. If you believe in it, it's quite a hard thing to do."

"Living in sin, from the point off view of the Church, but keeping in touch with heaven." Julia was angry. "I'm not going to demand any sacrifices from you. There's a hell of a lot of pride mixed up in sacrifice anyway. Both those alternatives are illogical and lunatic."

"And you think these two wildly inaccurate adjectives contain all the answers?"

She turned on him, then looked past him at a patch of sudden sunlight on the hundreds of examination papers varnished over the wall behind his young but absurdly apostolic head. They seemed to shine like a halo. "Don't you see that that's what we've been doing anyway? First we lived together, and you hovered miserably round the Mass. Then we stopped, and you went back while we waited for this annulment."

Paul said nothing, annoyed by her ruthless precision.

"Excuse me, but I couldn't help overhearing," said the gaunt young man at the next table. Julia swung round. "There's a story in Saint Thomas which might interest you." He leant forward solicitously. "It's about a man who decided that technically—I need not tell you the details—his marriage was not a marriage at all. He refused to—er—do his duty by his wife, and in due course she sued him for restitution of conjugal rights." The young man's voice was a drab monotone. "The Church refused him the Sacrament unless he restored those rights to his wife. Saint Thomas' comment"—his tone was suddenly triumphant—"is that it is better to be excommunicated than to commit fornication."

Julia was furious.

"How dare you. You—you—" She couldn't even find a word. "And next time you eavesdrop, at least listen more carefully," she added, having just grasped the point of the story. "It isn't even a relevant parallel."

"God bless you, God bless you," the young man muttered and went back to his studies. Julia turned to Paul, who looked embarrassed.

"In spite of the meaning of the word *alter*," she said, "there are usually three alternatives. You've already tried the first two—without the blessing of the civil courts of course, which means nothing to you. The third is to go our separate ways. I assume that what you were really trying to suggest was that."

"You have a way of putting things."

"Look, Paul, if you wanted a tender scene, full of noble sacrifice and protestations of eternal love, you can indulge elsewhere. You need the Sacraments more than you need me, okay, go ahead."

A roar of communal laughter leapt from the alcove and subsided. Paul looked as if the lion of that laughter had torn him apart and spat him out.

"Religion isn't something one *needs*, like a Horlicks drink for night starvation. Nor is love. They simply *are*. Oh, hell," he said miserably, "we don't even seem to talk the same language."

"Ah! Said the philologist fluent in Sanuri!" Julia was nearer to crying than she cared to show. "You of all men should understand other people's way of putting things. But perhaps you're right. We don't speak the same language. I thought we did." A sob rose in her throat as she got up, with eyes closed to keep back the tears. But she walked to the door steadily. The theology student was plunged in the *Summa* and did not look up.

## Chapter Five

**G**EORGINA RAYMOND had decorated her Soho flat in a Japanese style, that is to say, without furniture. "Can't afford it," she declared when she had first moved in on her return from Tokyo two years before. But in fact it must have cost her a tidy sum to adapt the first floor of an old Victorian house, with its ornamental chimney piece, cornices and French windows, to an Oriental simplicity.

A false ceiling of wide boards, not, alas of crytomeria but of ordinary stained timber, had been suspended, held on the underside by narrow strips of wood placed parallel to each other; the double door between the two rooms had been replaced by a sliding screen of papered panels, behind which a *tatami*, or bare bed of bamboo strips, had been built into the floor: the quilted bedding for it could unroll from the wall. The floor in both rooms was covered with wadded mats, arranged symmetrically. All the walls consisted of built-in cupboards, stained again to match the ceiling, except for the recess on the left of the chimney-breast, which Georgina had turned into a *tokonoma*. It was, luckily, fairly deep, and she had raised the floor there three inches, for the ceremonial effect. A flower arrangement stood in a vase on a low lacquered stand: before it, an incense burner on the floor, behind it, a single poem on a long scroll. But the chimney had been a problem: the *chigai-dana*, or shelves of uneven height, were supposed to be next to the *tokonoma*, separated only by a ceremonial post of gnarled wood, supporting the canopy as nature's contrasting contribution to the man-made straight lines and planes. Georgina had solved this brilliantly by pretending that the chimney piece wasn't there, building her irregular black shelves over and under it, blocking the fire-place, and continuing them into the other recess, where they became much deeper. The shelves contained only a few ornaments and books, for everything else was hidden away in sliding cupboards. One low shelf contained two bars of electric fire as a concession to the English winter; she could hardly have a charcoal brazier let into the floor. With fanatical perseverance, however, she had got hold of a slim trunk of young oak for the ceremonial post, which stood by the *tokonoma*, adding to its depth. The French windows she had had to leave, but they were screened by wide printed curtains imitating a stand of split bamboo. Square red cushions were arranged on the floor all round the room, and there was one small and very low wooden table from which to eat. The bathroom and kitchen, however, were entirely European.

Georgina had spent several years in the British Embassy in Tokyo. She had fallen in love with a smooth and unusually tall Japanese, and returned, unhappy but undaunted, to purse her studies of the language in London University. And all this was now rather out of date, for there she had met Hussein.

Zen-Buddhism had gone overboard for the Koran easily enough: she no longer sat cross-legged with her feet crooked under each knee, meditating on *nu*. But she could hardly change her interior decoration and purism forbade her to mix two styles.

Hussein, however, was most taken with it. He loved the cushions on the floor, and would crouch for hours chanting epics about tribal wars, or about Imam Abdul, the Leader, and his horse Garodi. He often brought his Sanuri friends, from the East End and from the Technical School, and they would accompany him, chanting too and drumming quick rhythms with their nails on a large wooden cigarette box, on the backs of saucepans, or on the cupboard walls. Hussein also liked her smooth red hair and her tall slim body. He responded to her taste for Oriental subtlety and the indirect poetic way of approaching serious subjects. And sometimes he sang a love-poem, sadly and in farewell. But she had not got around to learning very much Sanuri yet.

Georgina's parties were very literary. She wrote poetry, which was always accepted by the most reputable weeklies and periodicals; her translations of *haiku* were elegant, her own verse traditional and sensuous. She lived, partly on a Government grant and partly on reviews, neat short stories and articles about Japanese life and letters; and she had recently published two mock-pedantic essays on the misuse of the Chinese ideogram in the poetry of Ezra Pound.

Although she no longer expected her guests to take their shoes off in the hall, or to come through the door on their hands and knees, Georgina was considered eccentric by the literary types, who, contrary to the myth they liked to set up, were not in the least eccentric themselves, but hard workers, with families to support on a regular output of criticism, non-fiction books about their pet period, anthologies and long feature programmes for the BBC. Their well-earned reward, their idea of relaxation, was omniscience, not so much in scholarship, about which they were unnecessarily humble, but in literary gossip: who had reviewed what and where and who lived with whom. Georgina didn't care about these things at all, but they liked her, as an image of enthusiasm and irresponsibility through which they secretly fulfilled their own hankerings.

The room was ideal for a stand-up cocktail party: all the floor cushions had been removed from their ceremonial positions and stacked up in a corner, for the benefit of those guests who might later be overcome by drink and by the flabby English desire to paw and fondle. Some of the smaller sliding cupboards were opened, revealing shelves for ashtrays, cigarettes, and glasses; and a higher table had been imported from the kitchen to carry the regiment of bottles. The party was in full swing when Julia arrived.

"Darling! How are you? Where's Paul?"

"He'll be coming later, I expect," said Julia, prepared for this yet embarrassed. "He had some work to do. Hello, Hussein."

"Help yourself to a drink, I can't look after everyone." Georgina moved off with a bottle. Julia weaved her way to the table, followed by Hussein, who was looking anxious.

"Tell me, Hussein, have you seen Paul? Is he coming?"

"Julia," he said softly, "you suffer, too? Love is like the calf of a cow. Now he looks for you, now he runs away."

She poured herself a glass of white wine. "So he told you?"

"Yes, a little. I asked because I did not see you. A man who has not learnt why has not learnt anything."

"I see him everywhere, in the way a stranger walks in the street, in the cut of someone's hair on the back of his neck in a bus. I hear him in the things people say and in every book I try to read." She handed him some pineapple juice. "Is it like that with you, Hussein?"

"It is not the same, because I see her. But it will be the same, when I go back. Only the women at home, they will not remind me. They are beautiful, like the charcoal of the magag-tree. But her skin is the white of the plateau, her eyes are blue berries, and her hands are drops of rain. Her hair is the tail of Imam Abdul's sorrel horse, who carries him away very fast."

"Hussein, what would happen if you married her and took her back with you?"

He looked deeply in to his glass of juice. "I cannot. My family will never see me. They sent already my brother-in-law and my cousin to tell me. My father forbids and in my country we cannot do against the father, it is written."

"But she would become a Moslem."

"There are three things with us in marriage, all very strong: the money, with the house and the camels; the tribe or race; and the religion. My father married an Isharood and that was not very good, but the money was all right, and the religion. My friend married a West African and he can never go back. Our race shines the best, like the diamond," he added, with complete conviction, which strangely mingled both arrogance and naiveté.

"I suppose all these ties are too strong for you to stay here with her?" A slightly bitter note crept into her gentleness.

"I cannot go through the window when there is a door," he said, "or climb in secret over a fence of thorns when there is an open path. If my father forbids, and I do, I must abandon my religion."

Julia froze for a moment, then drained her glass quickly. "Did Paul tell you if he'd be coming tonight?"

"He said no, he would not. I am very sorry, Julia. It is bad, yes, but it is good also. Look at the thing and the thing beyond it."

"I know. It's my fault, anyway."

"We have a story. There was a time when work did itself, and all the burdens, they carried themselves. But one day a woman was impatient, because the burdens went too slow. So she picked them up and carried them herself." He sipped his fruit juice thoughtfully for a moment, as if the English words he wanted might be dissolved in it. "The other burdens were all jealous and wanted to be carried also. They—how do you say—put themselves on the strike. And the men were so angry with the woman, that ever since that day they have made the woman carry all the burdens."

Julia laughed despite her gloom. "Do you think it's true, Hussein?"

"The men, they have their burdens also. Probably those who refused to be on the strike."

"We call them blacklegs."

"Black legs?" Hussein looked puzzled, but pursued his idea. "Those burdens with black legs perhaps continued to carry themselves, and then they were punished by the others and given up to the men, who carry them very badly." He sighed, then smiled suddenly. "Here is Mister Jacob, with his angel."

Justin Jacob had edged up towards him, but carefully addressed himself to Julia as he spoke. "Hello, Hussein. Who's the charming lady?"

Hussein introduced them.

"And what do you do for your green eyes? Are you a writer, too?"

She was playing with the curls behind her ear. "I'm afraid not. Actually, I'm doing nothing, just resting after a monumental PhD thesis."

"Oh? What's it on?"

Julia laughed uncertainly. "Don't ask, or I'll start telling you."

"No, really, I want to know. I might want to publish it."

"Oh? Who are you?"

"I'm at Tweedie and Tweedie. We're fairly anxious to get some scholarly books on our list." He smiled pleasantly at Hussein, to keep him there.

"You won't want this." She accepted a cigarette.

Hussein refused one politely and said, "Julia is as clever as a monkey." Then Georgina fetched him away, to Justin's chagrin. Then he pursued his business as a talent-scout. "Tell me all the same."

"Well, it's on mediaeval religious poetry." She made it as vague as possible. Then accuracy got the better of her. "Chiefly William of Shoreham. Kentish," she added with a neurotic compulsion, though it hardly seemed relevant. Justin raised a querying eyebrow and she warmed to her old subject in spite of herself. "I was tracing the influence of the liturgy on thirteenth and fourteenth century religious lyrics. It was—but don't let me be a bore."

"But that sounds fascinating." Behind the conventional party phrase he was genuinely interested. "Just the sort of book we'd like to publish. Can you send me a synopsis of it?"

"Well, I could. But I honestly don't think it's publishable. It's all cluttered with footnotes. You know what thesis style is—writing with only three people and their particular objections in mind."

"Of course. We've seen several of them. But you could rewrite it, more simply."

"I don't know. I have to get a job soon."

"Look, in your own good time, send me a specimen rewritten chapter and a synopsis, and if we like it we'll commission it. You can always do it as well as a job. Most people do."

"Darling Julia," Georgina broke in. "Don't be so serious. You always get into such earnest conversations at my parties. Where's Paul? Everyone's having fun, look."

Julia smiled, more happily than she had done for some time, and obediently looked through the shifting kaleidoscope of party dresses, dark suits and colourful ties, to the pile of red cushions now hidden by three necking couples; the sliding screen between the rooms was open and floor-level bed of springy bamboo was similarly occupied. A well-known critic lay full length on the floor, balancing a glass on his belly. She shut her eyes for a moment and listened to the soundtrack, which seemed like a police chase through a giant hen-coop, punctuated by the sort of whish-hooting noise that accompanies destroyers firing out in British films. Among the guests still standing, names were being thrown up above the hubbub, usually with a knowledgeable and derogatory coda: "Bergsonism, and all that" "Hesse? Oh well, the Germans dive very deep and come up very muddy..." "Simone de Beauvoir—oh yes. Notre Dame De Sartre, what?" "Well, I'm an illogical positivist, so there."

She saw Hussein, towering over a small group of impressionable students. He was always a little bewildered by Georgina's parties, especially towards the end. But he knew she never let anyone fondle her: she had explained to him the "everything but" attitude of the Anglo-Saxon world, and she herself, without seeming in the least prudish, had a *noli me tangere* look which people respected.

The students were having an animated discussion. Julia joined them. "We have a proverb," Hussein was saying with a dazzling smile, "the outsider claps his hands but nothing moves."

There was a roar of laughter. Hussein, puzzled by his success, turned to Julia. "They laugh at me?"

"No, Hussein. They're pleased with your proverb."

He nodded happily. "It's a good proverb. And you? You are not so unhappy?"

"No, I feel much better. But I think I'll go home, now, I'm very tired."

"I will take you."

"She smiled at him gratefully. "But wouldn't you rather stay with Georgina?"

"I will take you. Maybe I come back. Maybe I go home also."

Incongruously enough in those Far Eastern surroundings, Georgina had taken out a guitar and was sitting on the low bed, leaning against two bodies and strumming rather obvious harmonies to American Negro spirituals and extracts from *Porgy and Bess*.

"I'll ring her tomorrow to thank her," said Julia. They slipped away into the night.

## Chapter Six

WHEN Julia got back to her room she lay on her bed, slightly tipsy, and smoked a cigarette. She never drank very much, but it always went to her head. She felt maudlin, and cried a little, but for the first time in a week, she was not unhappy. Although she knew that tomorrow she would be missing Paul in every fibre, she felt, for the moment, indifferent. 'To hell with it,' she thought, and indulged in a vision of herself having published an important book of criticism, reading her reviews, going to literary parties. But it wouldn't be that sort of book. It would be too clever. She thought of Georgina, a wit among scholars and a scholar among wits, and envied her poise. Georgina seemed to take everything in her stride, even absolute enthusiasms, even the knowledge that these didn't last, even Hussein.

Julia smiled to herself happily. She would be like Georgina, from now on. She picked up a magazine called *Scopes and Horoscopes*, and turned to Aquarius:

> *I do not like the main outlook on friendships and general emotional interests in May. Firm handling of your own reactions will be required. On the other hand, projects which have until now seemed slow in bearing fruit receive encouragement from unexpected quarters. Yet do not allow pessimism arising out of slackening trends to delude you into hasty ventures...*

At this moment, her bell rang. She looked at the clock with surprise. It was ten to twelve. 'Paul!' she thought, and raced downstairs. There was a street lamp just outside, shedding its misty light upon a shorter, bulkier figure than Paul's, in a duffel coat: Bernard Reeves was swaying slightly. His Lambretta lurched drunkenly against the pavement.

"Hello," he mumbled. "I thought I'd see how you were. I've just been to a party."

"So've I," she said idiotically, to gain time.

"Can I come in a moment?"

"Well, it's rather late." She heard her own voice being rather priggish, and wanted to add, nonchalantly, "just for a minute, then," but felt that would sound unnecessarily cautious. So she said, "I've got no drink to offer you, I'm afraid."

They went upstairs quietly. He hardly noticed the room. He was looking at her intensely, recognising the same low cut black dress she had worn at Angela's party, and the same fine gold crucifix.

"You've been crying. I just knew you were miserable, and alone. I just knew."

"You seem to know a hell of a lot."

"I met Angela Kriss and you cropped up in the conversation." He suddenly looked rather miserable himself. "In fact, I made her talk about you, I wanted her to talk about you. She told me your engagement was broken off." He put it in the passive, tactfully.

"So, everyone seems to know a hell of a lot." She flopped down in the armchair near the bed and motioned him to the other. But he put his duffel coat on it instead and sat on the bed, leaning towards her.

"I just knew you were miserable," he repeated hypnotically, and took her hand. She withdrew it, rather puzzled. He was obviously drunk.

"Look, I'm not miserable, I've been to a splendid party and I feel fine." Her voice suddenly trembled on the last word.

"Why have you been crying then?" he asked gently, putting his hand on hers again.

"I haven't been crying." And she burst into tears.

He drew her up towards him and put her head on his shoulder. She wept bitterly for a moment, then felt foolish, which made her weep a little more.

"Use me," he intoned, "use me as a cushion." She found herself smiling through her sobs. He really was rather ridiculous. "You just need to look after you for a bit and take you out of yourself."

"But—why are you doing this?" she looked up and wiped her tears.

"Because I care for you. Nothing more. No strings attached." He still had his arm round her and rocked her gently, which made her want to giggle. She had always disliked the euphemistic approach, and wasn't taken in for a moment. But suddenly she was overcome with a longing for Paul, and started crying again.

"It's so stupid," she sobbed, "I made him break off myself."

"There, my sweet. Talk about it. Cry all you want. Use me," he murmured, stroking her hair.

"And now—I can't bear—being shut out. We were such good friends. It's that I miss most."

"Were you—living together?" Bernard asked with studied casualness. He was much more sober now.

"That's just it. We had been, then we didn't." She felt horrified at suddenly confiding in him and stopped. "Oh, it's a long story. His religion came into it." She heard the dissociating adjective "his" with mild surprise. "That's why I can't understand it—just because we can't marry. It's so humiliating." Her left hand was buried into the back of her hair, combing it out with quick nervous movements. "When a man's in love, he loves everything. And then nothing. No interest at all." She started crying again, overwhelmed with self-pity that was now mingled with shame at her lack of discretion. He gave her his handkerchief.

"Blow your nose, there's a good girl."

"I must look awful."

He stroked her hair again. "You couldn't if you tried. That man Paul must be out of his mind."

The tears welled up again at the mention of his name. She forgot the insincerity of his compliment in her desire both to defend Paul and to unburden herself. "He's a Catholic. You see, I've been married before."

His interest perked up visibly. Julia was too upset to remember that any avowal of marital complications, past or present, is usually interpreted as a tacit admission of availability: that a certain type of woman, in fact, used confession as a means of ensnaring a certain type of man.

"Oh, it only lasted six months," she went on between sniffs. "I was eighteen. Just after the war in Germany. We had nothing in common but the Intercomm."

He gave her a cigarette and she tapped it nervously on the back of her hand. He rested his fingers on hers when he gave her a light, and she was aware of his eye on her décolleté as she leant forward. "The Catholic position is a bit ruthless, I must say."

"Oh, I agree with the Church's general stand on divorce. It's the subtle twists in the Canon Law I can't take. Some people get annulments, others don't. I've been told there's no doubt whatsoever that my marriage wasn't a marriage in the Catholic sense, but it can't be proved legally. And if it could, I wouldn't believe in an annulment which depended on such machinations." She was grinding her axe, partly out of latent anger, and partly to make her own moral attitude clear. "If someone had told me all this at the time I wouldn't have gone through with it. I've always had an instinctive knowledge that I would one day want to become a Catholic, but later rather than sooner. You know how the war affected everybody, one lived in the present. I simply thought, if it didn't work out, we'd split up."

"Are you going to become a Catholic?" he asked carefully.

She puffed at her cigarette, and put it out, half-smoked. "No," she said at last. He looked relieved. "I think the Church is wrong on this point. And one can't be a Catholic and think the Church is wrong." She was playing with her hair again and he watched her fingers as the wisps curled round them. "They say that any marriage outside the Church is a marriage in the Catholic sense unless proved otherwise. But few people know what that means nowadays, unless they're inside the Church to begin with. I think the wording should be changed to 'no marriage outside the Church is a marriage in the Catholic sense unless proved to be so'."

Bernard was still a little too befuddled to give even a layman's *nihil obstat* to her proposed amendment to Canon Law. He stubbed his cigarette out and took her hand again. "It's strange, I thought from the subject that you were a Catholic. I suppose one can't be a mediaevalist without getting tinged."

"Well, I did get very near, through Paul."

His name seemed to be a valve-opener.

"Use my shoulder," he said gently, "it's there when you want it."

She did want it, but after a while began to think: 'oh, hell, what am I doing? This man is too silly for words.' It was natural enough to blame his silliness for her confessional self-indulgence. She sat up again and

*The Languages of Love: Chapter Six*

glanced at him. He suddenly looked rather old and flabby. She gazed down at the floor, reflecting that the more blasé and self-assured a man seemed, the more sentimental and gauche he was likely to be.

"Look, don't go and fall in love with me, Bernard." The sentence sounded absurd, and she realised that this was the first time she had used his Christian name. "Because I just can't cope at the moment."

"Who said I was in love with you?" he picked up *Scopes and Horoscopes* and fingered through its pages. His was certainly an approach she wasn't used to, and he played it hard.

"No-one," she said, feeling a little foolish. "I'm just telling you, don't."

"I only want to help you, to be around if you want someone to talk to, someone to take you out a bit." A question, 'where does your wife come into all this', rose in her mind, to be said rather solemnly. But he was obviously a relatively free agent, and suddenly she felt very tired, indifferent to him and to everyone else. She let her head flop back on his shoulder and closed her eyes. He raised a little the arm that was supporting her and smoothed her brow with his hand. He put down the magazine as if he had found therein all the platitudes he needed.

"Don't forget that you're probably run down anyway, after all the work you've been doing. Things aren't quite so bad. Use me, my dear, use me." He was evidently fond of this refrain, perhaps he had prepared the technique and didn't want to forget about it. "And now, with no strings attached," he repeated, "no obligations at all, kiss me."

Her first reaction was one of meek obedience to a tutor's advice, and she dutifully gave him her lips for a gentle, friendly kiss. Then irrationally, she felt curious about him, wanting him to betray his motives. Her tongue crept into his mouth and explored it deeply. She put her arms round him, ruffling the fair hair at the back of his neck. He gave a little moan and held her more closely, modelling her breasts with his hand. She experienced not a twinge of desire.

They disentangled themselves and looked at each other, she smiling ironically, he rather sheepishly. She tried to look pleased instead of amused. He tried to look bluff.

"Who taught you to kiss like that?" he asked lightly. "I see what you mean by your warning. You little devil." He seemed to have difficulty in keeping his hands off her. "But don't worry," he added with an unnaturally casual laugh, "I can look after myself, and you."

He got up. She handed him his coat. "Give me your telephone number," he said as if it couldn't matter less. "I'll give you a ring tomorrow and take you out to dinner. We can talk about the book."

She was faintly annoyed that he should so readily assume she would be free, but felt cynical enough not to care. When the rattle of his Lambretta had died away, she decided that he was a bore, that she had been an idiot, and that she would be otherwise engaged tomorrow. By the time she had got undressed, the thought she might as well take him at his word and use him, if only to go out a little, if only, she exploded the covering phrase with devastating honesty, to flirt a little, to tempt him, to be wanted.

She lay awake in bed, disliking herself and thinking of Paul.

## Chapter Seven

PROFESSOR JARVIS-ANDERSON lived in Hampstead, in a rambling Victorian red-brick house which nevertheless seemed far too small, not only for his own bulk but for his untidily sprawling family. His wife, Marion Farquharson, was a successful novelist who had produced five large family sagas and five large children, though John Jarvis-Anderson never seemed quite sure how many there were of either. The children certainly sounded more numerous. He had, rather cruelly, named them after Anglo-Saxon and Old Norse heroes, and they often behaved as belligerently: there were four boys, Hrothgar, Wiglaf, Kári and Njàl, and one girl, Hildigunn, all as yet under twelve. John Jarvis-Anderson liked to imagine that they were acquiring, by the magic of nomenclature, some of the characteristics of their namesakes: that Hrothgar, the eldest, was wise, Wiglaf loyal; that Hildigunn, who came next, was proud, Kári steadfast and ruthless, while Njàl, who was only four, was surely gifted with second sight. Perhaps all these qualities were there, lost in the hectic exuberance of life, but so far the children seemed most alike in one thing above all, their love of noise.

Marion, however, was regally imperturbable, a fit heroine for any saga. She ran the house with a quiet efficiency, behind the chaos and between long bouts of typing when even the appearance of a dragon breathing fire would not have interrupted her. Laconic and direct in speech, voluble in her writing, she seemed to have herself and life under happy control, never letting her work interfere with the much more important business of adoring her husband and his heroic offspring.

Julia felt immediately at ease with them, at least, as soon as she met Marion. The professor had opened the door himself and taken her into the drawing-room, which looked more like an Oxford tutor's study and was littered with galley-proofs. He himself, far from being as fierce as he had seemed at her viva, was quietly polite. He talked with a shy smile and a nervous forward shrug of his left shoulder.

"Have a strong Martini and meet my wife," he said as they went in, with only the slightest pause between the two suggestions. "My dear, this is Miss Grampion. Be kind to her: she looks very tired."

"I'm always kind to your students, it's my job." Marion laughed. "Have to be, after you've dealt with them."

Julia sat down and relaxed, for the first time, it seemed, in weeks. She looked at Marion as they talked, and liked her, without knowing who she was, simply as a professor's unusually handsome and lively wife. Most academic wives were lively enough, when they were not mousy, but in a jerky way, as if trying a little too hard to show that they had not been dulled by their husbands, or, if they were academic in their own right, by the double dose of scholarship. But Marion was lively in a peaceful way. Her pale blond hair matched her husband's, though his had more white in it and was coarser. She wore it drawn smoothly back in a tressed coil on the top of her head. She was statuesque: Julia wanted to curtsey and kiss her hand; but he was a shaggy polar bear, and huggable.

The professor was showing her a new photograph of a famous crux in a manuscript. "Of course, ultra-violet ray is not synonymous with truth. It makes you look at the manuscript too long." He smiled gently but his tone was mischievously ironical. "Its only advantage is that it shows you forms you would otherwise never have thought of as linguistically possible." He spoke with an almost imperceptible stammer which veiled his precision with an air of timid informality.

Julia silently invented a new linguistic group for him, and a chair to go with it, nominating him Professor of Hesitant Languages. "I'm a little worried about applying for this job, sir." She had no sense of salesmanship. "Philology's my weakest point, as you no doubt realised from my thesis."

"Ah, yes, I seem to remember a little jousting between us." He smiled benevolently.

"You can make anything your weakest point by thinking of it as such," Marion put in. Julia looked at her with surprise. "Don't forget that the lecturer can have his textual comments in front of him. I feel much more sympathy for the student."

*The Languages of Love: Chapter Seven*

"My wife is very wise. Those with the best memory get the firsts." Julia laughed, uncertain as to whether this was derogatory or not. "But you know the texts," he went on, "you must have done them yourself as an undergraduate."

"Of course." Julia felt she ought to leave it at that, but honesty was compellingly her worst policy. "I didn't mean that I couldn't comment on the texts, sir, only that if my heart wasn't in it I wouldn't do it imaginatively and stimulatingly. I'd rather talk about the poetry all the time."

"I remember a student asking me, at some gathering or other, if my subject was English Literature." The professor shrugged his shoulder forward gently and smiled. "I replied, yes, Anglo-Saxon and Middle English. He said: 'No, I mean literature.' But then he was a Cambridge man."

Julia gazed at the palaeographic problem on the photograph. "I know one can't really divide form and content," she said, "but it's very difficult not to, the way things are presented. It's either all sound-change or it's all what the poet says and why he says it." She warmed to her own ideas and spoke quickly. "I'm interested in language as a process, not a thing or an essence. Phonetic laws are useful, I know, but they aren't fixed laws, like the laws of nature. You can't say that a hard *c* before a palatal *a* will inevitably soften to *ch*: in Southern and Central France it did, in Northern France it didn't. So we have castle from the Normans and chastity from Parisian French two centuries later."

"Which is odd in itself, don't you think?" said Marion.

"Philology is not a science, Miss Grampion," said the professor benignly. "It is an art, borrowing from science. One has to remember each fact separately, and make up the pattern for each language or dialect, or class, or even each individual."

"I know, but philologists do tend to talk of Grimm's Law as if a Primitive Germanic Assembly had passed it, ordering everyone to pronounce their *p*s as *b*s and their *t*s as *d*s from then on."

"Sounds grim to me." Marion laughed. "Have another drink, will you?"

"I beg your pardon." The professor hurried forward to fill her glass. "I was thinking of a much nicer consonant shift they had in Finnish and Hungarian. Yes," he mused, waving the cocktail shaker gently in the air, "it really is quite the nicest consonant shift I know."

"John dear, do stick to the point."

"Of course, my dear. Miss Grampion is right. It is the individual styles of language which spread through imitation. There is no such thing as a great anonymous mass movement of sounds—or indeed of ideas."

"But why is it all presented as if there was?"

"The linguist can only know the state of a language when the individual style is generalised. It is in a constant state of flux, there are no real boundaries or unified communities, and mingling continues through supra-political or social bonds." He paused as Julia looked puzzled. "No language or dialect is free from alien influence. There is no limit to the possibility of speech-blending, no limit at all." The prospect sent him into a reverie.

"It's the purely fortuitous character of sound-change that I find so disconcerting," Julia began, and was unexpectedly proved right by a sudden degringolating noise from the stairs. A dirty little face, topped by a tousle of straight fair hair, peered around the door.

"Daddy, can I borrow the Anglo-Saxon dictionary? We're building a fort and the Oxford ones aren't enough."

"I thought I told you to go and have your bath," said Marion placidly. "Well, now you're here, come in and say how do you do to Miss Grampion —or can I call you Julia? This is Hrothgar."

Julia thought he looked more like Ulf the Unwashed. She smiled. "Where's your fort? Is it very big?"

"It's at the top of the stairs. Nobody can get by, nobody at all."

"But who is Nobody? He must be a very fierce enemy."

Hrothgar was enchanted with this. "He's a giant, and he has lots of heads." He started improvising loudly. "He has as many heads as the dictionary's got words. That's why we're building a fort with them, to frighten him."

Julia laughed. "You mean all the words will rattle out, like ammunition, and snap off each head?"

Hrothgar thought for a minute. "No, they're death-rays. Every word's a death-ray!" And he jumped about happily, making shooing noises.

"Well, don't wake up Njàl," said Marion, "and I'll be up in half an hour to put you all to bed, so you'd better kill off Nobody before then."

"I'm Somebody, the bravest of the brave!" shouted Hrothgar, marching up to his father. "Can I take the dictionary, daddy please?"

John Jarvis-Anderson smiled, with great affection. "If you don't tear it to pieces."

"Oh, no! it's only for the top tower, I promise." He rushed to a lower shelf and struggled to lift the two heavy volumes of Bosworth and Toller.

"Here, I'll carry them up for you," Julia offered, "that is, if I'm allowed near your fort. I might be Nobody's spy, for all you know."

Hrothgar considered this solemnly. He could manage the volumes, but only in two journeys, and the operation was urgent. He solved the problem with a triumphant smile. "You're Somebody's Faithful Friend," he said simply. "Come on."

When Julia re-entered the drawing-room a few minutes later, she felt very serene. This family, she thought, would no doubt seem donnishly whimsical as an epigram, casually met but intricately made, which suddenly causes everything else, however irrelevant, to fall into place. Even phonology seemed worthwhile now, whispering the sounds of time into the very material that poets used, the vowels jealously mutating, angrily fracturing as consonant groups shifted to their conditioned cues in wild adenoidal ecstasies. The flesh and bones of words rose again to the salvation of their etymologies. And the job he was telling her about seemed interesting and desirable, the academic world was human, sane, honest, and kind, its values were respected and, as far as any could be on this side of paradise, absolute. She wanted, desperately, to fit in, to possess this little world, to love it. Paul belonged to it, and loved it, in his own way. He fitted in. It allowed for the infinite variety of human eccentricity. Bernard, she vaguely felt, did not truly belong, for it ruthlessly rejected even the slightly spurious. It might, very easily, reject her.

She had rung up the professor that morning and had been delighted when he invited her for the very same day, so that she could quite truthfully claim to be engaged when Bernard had asked her out to dinner. He had not pressed her to another definite date.

"Well, now you know more about it, " said Jarvis-Anderson, "and what your chances are, I do hope you will apply. As you see, it's not all mnemonic philology."

Julia smiled. "I'm very flattered. And I shall certainly apply. How long do you think it will take, I mean, before they decide on someone?" This time it was the professor, not Bernard, who was unconsciously excluded from the jury in the pronoun "they".

"The applications have to be in by the end of this week." He filled her glass again. "The job was advertised some time ago and quite a few have come in already. We shall be interviewing the best candidates at the beginning of June: the successful one would hear, I suppose, about a week later."

In spite of his encouragement, Julia felt she didn't stand much of a chance. She ran her fingers through the back of her hair. "Even if I did get it, I shall have to take a temporary job for the summer. My grant stops in June."

Marion looked at her. "You don't want to spend the next two months in an office or in a summer school. After all that hard work you must start fresh. Perhaps I can get you some reviewing."

"Reviewing?" Julia was puzzled.

"Oh, you know, travel books, deep-sea diving, tiger-hunting. Not to mention biographies, criticism, and novels. All the semi-literary crap that pours out of publishers' presses in a weekly cataract."

"But why should I—"

"It's not very well paid, of course, but it's easy work, and if you do enough of it and live simply, you can get by."

"I mean, how can you—"

"I've been writing enormous average novels for ten years. I know most of the literary editors and they treat me fairly enough. Marion Farquharson, that's me."

Julia was astonished. "I didn't know. I'm sorry, how stupid of me." In spite of Marion's dismissing gesture, she felt embarrassed and added quickly, "but I couldn't review books. I don't seem to have read anything after 1400 for years."

There was a shout upstairs. Marion took no notice. "My dear girl, you could do it standing on your head. I've done it myself and I'm not even intelligent."

"I should think anyone could review the sort of book my wife has mentioned," the professor qualified carefully.

"Besides," Marion went on, "your training in research must have taught you to gut a book in half an hour."

"That sort of book," the professor repeated, and seemed a little incredulous as to its possible existence.

"Well—" Julia looked doubtful. She never gutted a book in half an hour, but took detailed notes for several days. "It's very kind of you. I suppose there's no harm in trying. But haven't they all got their regular contributors?"

Marion smiled. "Yes, of course. But even journalists go on holidays, you know. Mind you, that cuts both ways, it's also the silly season in publishing. Still, I'll have a word with Desmond Sykes, and perhaps a few others."

Julia's eye had been wandering round the room while Marion talked. Suddenly she yelped with delight. "Oh! You've got a harpsichord. Is it yours?"

Marion laughed "Not entirely. We couldn't afford it. So John gave me half a harpsichord and I gave him half a harpsichord." The logic seemed irrefutable.

"It was made," said the professor, "by a friend of ours, so we paid a little less. He was quite good at Chinese, but his real passion in life was making harpsichords. We sometimes play four-hands, my wife and I."

The idea of those two sitting together at that small and delicate instrument sent Julia into peals of laughter. John and Marion joined in. They were all laughing when a prolonged rumble, followed by loud swift thumps and much screaming, compelled their attention. The entire fort, and at least one of the warriors, must have fallen down the stairs. A brief silence was broken by yells of pain. Julia rushed to the door.

"It's Wiglaf," said Marion calmly. "I really must get them to bed. Heavens, it's eight o'clock, you must be starving."

"I'll come and help you."

"You sit down and talk shop with John. They're excited enough without Somebody's Faithful Friend putting them to bed. Dinner'll be ready in half an hour. I'm so sorry." And with this unexpected apology for what was obviously going to be the most efficiently organised of half-hours, she sailed out, majestic and bow-fronted as a Viking ship.

## Chapter Eight

LIKE the tree in the quad, the British Museum Reading Room seemed to exist only when one turned up there oneself. After an absence of several weeks, it was difficult to believe that it could have gone on, for the benefit of so many other scholars, so many critics, poets, paupers and eccentrics, hatchers of revolutions, unravellers of genealogies, authors of pamphlets or of long begging letters to the Royal Family. Yet there it still stood, round and reassuring as the womb, its enormous floor starred by concentric seats, all pointing to the circular shelves of catalogues and the little circus of polite attendants and superintendents who waited, like patient performers, for the extraordinary demands of the great enquiring public. There it continued, highly domed as an observatory, busy as a beehive and honeycombed with books, surrounded behind the scenes by twisting galleries, subterranean corridors and Freudian spiral staircases, smelling mustily of books, and books, and more books. Its corked floor silenced the constant footsteps, but there was a continuous murmur of voices, punctuated by thuds as catalogues were replaced, and by the frequent ringing of quiet telephones, long whispered conversations in foreign tongues, giggling glamorous Italian girls here to prepare bibliographies for their professors whose temporary mistresses they might well be, and, alas, by the nattering of English old maids, who advertised for research work of any kind in the weekly periodicals.

It was impossible to go there without meeting at least three acquaintances, people who, like the Reading Room itself, did not exist except in one's awareness of that context. But sometimes one met a person who did exist—more persistently than was desirable in the consciousness of one's own emotions which continued, irrespective of scholars and cranks, outside the dreamlike procession of all those million volumes.

After a few weeks of inactivity, Julia suddenly returned, spurred to new undertakings. There was the chapter and synopsis to write for Justin Jacob, and texts to brush up in case of an interview, not to mention a desultory search for the treatment of adultery in mediaeval romances.

The first person she met was Paul, on the steps leading up to the columns that supported the monstrous pediment, from which a watchful female figure seemed to drop a great stone ball on every small, unwary seeker after Truth. He had just emerged, with his briefcase, and was lighting a cigarette. Behind his cupped hands the match lit up his face, unmistakably edged with black like a stained-glass saint, outlined in lead. Her heart seemed to leap into her throat. She couldn't avoid him, and didn't want to, but she felt a rush of blood to her face, followed at once by cold, prickly sweat.

"Hello, Paul. I thought you didn't smoke in the morning?"

He looked embarrassed. "Well, I do a bit, now." There was a pause. "Have one?"

Her hand trembled as she held the cigarette for him to light. "How are you?"

"Oh, all right," he replied. "Working hard. Hussein's in there, I've been showing him how to use the catalogues. You might help him if he gets into difficulties with tickets."

"Yes, of course." She wanted to ask, had he missed her, did he still like her, couldn't they meet now and again, simply as friends? But space and time lingered over his face like a veil she couldn't lift. They seemed to have nothing to say to each other. They walked up and down the colonnade.

"What are you doing?" he asked awkwardly after a moment's silence. She told him, grateful for a subject, about the possible job, the possible book, leaving out, without quite knowing why, the possible contribution on adultery. He said he was very glad.

"So you see, I may be around in the academic world. We'll probably bump into each other." She glanced up at him, the unspoken words racing round her head—'Paul, can't we be civilised about this, not shut each other out so completely, break it off gently, oh darling, it's only by seeing you as a friend that I can stop thinking of you like this, you've become an obsession—' She said aloud, "I hope you don't object."

He gave her a strained look. "It's upsetting, of course. I thought I'd put you out of mind." The words slashed into the lump in her throat, releasing hot tears that filled her eyes in an instant. "Seeing you makes me realise how I've missed you." It was the other way with her. She blinked hard to dry her eyelashes. "You're looking very beautiful," he added softly.

She felt herself relax, and smiled. Just to have him there, tender and personal again, even for a moment, made her feel she hadn't missed him all that much, or wouldn't any more. "Well, I'm sorry about this." She forced a note of gaiety into her voice. "I'll try and keep out of your way."

"No, don't do that. Don't avoid me." His tone was anxious and his eyes intense. Then the veil dropped over them again as the flicker of despair gave way to male common sense. "I mean, as you say, we're bound to meet now and again. I expect I'll get used to it." He smiled. "Each time will be a bit easier."

"Yes, you'll get used to it," she echoed, hurt by his selfishness, momentary though she knew it to be. "Well, I must go in and do some work. Goodbye." With an effort she added, "nice to have seen you." She felt the lump rise in her throat again and wanted to turn away, but stayed fixed to the spot like one of the columns. He did not similarly qualify his goodbye, though he smiled and nodded before hurrying down the steps. She gazed after him, unable to move, following his tall figure as it turned left outside the gates and flicked quickly along beyond the high railings, as shot from an old film-reel, until he was out of sight.

The ex-guardsman at the door of the Reading Room greeted her with Irish exuberance, but she didn't feel like stopping. He would want to know all about her absence, if only as an excuse for trotting out the tall stories and small snapshots from his past career. She spotted Hussein at once, bent over the catalogues like a black question mark. But she wanted to compose herself first, and find somewhere to sit.

It was half past eleven and the room was very full. The entire staff of all the provincial universities of Britain seemed to have come to town, goaded to sudden research by the need for promotion. But the old regulars were there too: the lonely Pole who had made so many Approaches to Dostoievski; the bearded man who surreptitiously combed the long silky grey hair which fell halfway down his back, the purple-faced redhead in dark satin bloomer, green woolly socks and a man's blue blazer; the lecherous Indian who prowled around, eyeing the younger female readers with the measure of his courage.

After walking all the way round, Julia found a free seat at last, and put her handbag on the desk and her coat on the chair. The man on her right looked up. It was Bernard Reeves. He raised his eyebrows and smiled in recognition, obviously pleased as well as amused.

"I'm so sorry, I didn't see you," she whispered, "d'you mind if I sit here? There's nowhere else."

"I'm delighted. Come and have a coffee."

"I've just had one," she lied, "and it's so late, I'd better get down to some work."

"Lunch?"

She hesitated. A loud "shshsh" came from an angry bald man in the seat to the left of hers. In a flash she thought of dating up Hussein, just to annoy Bernard, but equally swiftly remembered that he had little money and would be going back to the Department Canteen. She nodded to Bernard and went off to the catalogues, feeling utterly lonely, knowing that today of all days she must not take him at his word and use him, precisely because she most needed him, or, indeed, anyone.

Hussein was having a splendid time with the catalogues, which seemed to contain few of the books he needed but millions he didn't need. He had already filled up thirty-two tickets for books on the most extraordinary subjects, all by authors whose names began with San—; they had caught his fancy while he was looking for British Government surveys of Sanuri. The motives behind all this were curiously mixed: Hussein, like most of his countrymen, could not believe in disinterested scholarship. Once he had satisfied himself that the University did in fact get money from the State, he knew that all this fantastic network of little rooms full of learned men who wanted to find out about muted-vowel vibrations or whatever was really being used by the British Government. "The hired man is never himself free," he would reply to Paul's protests. Hence his search for publications variously called *A General Survey of the Sanuri Protectorate, 1948-1950,* or *The Mineral Resources of the Sanuri Protectorate,* or *Report on the Tribes of Sanuri (1952).* And although his own curiosity could be so haphazardly aroused as to put in for all the novels of William Sansom, and his efforts to satisfy that curiosity completely disinterested, he saw no incongruity in his convictions.

"You can't put in for all those," said Julia, smiling at his childish, imaginative handwriting. "There's a limit to what they'll keep for you and you'll never read them all today."

Hussein looked regretfully at his pile of tickets. "It is very sad. I will ask for only this one, then, and these." These were two of the Surveys. This one was called *Are there Angels in Outer Space?* by P. Sanverino.

Bernard Reeves was watching her from his seat as she showed Hussein where to put his tickets. But when she finally returned after a long session at the catalogues, first for her own books, then chatting to Hussein again, he was very consciously buried in his books.

"Do you mind having lunch early? My books won't come for some time."

"Oh, it's you! Yes, by all means."

He helped her on with her coat. "Who's the Negro?" he asked casually as they came out of the swing-doors onto the porch.

"That's Hussein. He's not a Negro, he's an African. And in any case, he's a Hamite." She spoke a little angrily, feeling dispirited. This was where she had talked to Paul, and meeting Hussein had made it worse. But she was pleased by his curiosity, and volunteered no more than ethnographical information.

He took her to a smooth and soothing Turkish restaurant in Soho. The waiters were obsequious, the wine mellowed her, after a burst of artificial gaiety, into a mood of maudlin confidential introspection, followed unexpectedly by careless warmth and a sudden longing for tenderness.

"What you need at the moment," said Bernard with an affectionate twinkle in his blue eyes, "is a discreet and light-hearted love affair. And to be told several times a day that you're beautiful and attractive—and great fun to be with." He pressed his knees against hers under the table and took her hand, fingering it gently.

She frowned and played with her hair, annoyed to feel the first pang of desire singing through her veins, mild as yet but undoubtedly there, where it had not been. She attributed it to the wine and to her wretchness.

"No," she said slowly, "that's not what I need at all. Besides, these things can't be treated like cures, or drugs. One might get addicted," she paused, and added, by way of a red light, "you're no use to me. I want to be loved."

He looked deep into his empty coffee cup, still holding her hand, and said very softly, "I want to be loved, too."

## Chapter Nine

GEORGINA lay on her bamboo bed, leaning against the wall, with a white typewriter propped up on her knees and her red hair loose on her shoulders. The telephone, which was also white, was at the level of the bed, that is to say, on the matted floor, with an extra little painted mat all to itself. An empty coffee cup stood next to it. Georgina lifted the receiver and dialled.

"Hello, Julia? I saw Paul yesterday. Darling, I'm so sorry. How ever many bricks did I drop last Tuesday? No wonder you disappeared so early."

"I meant to ring you up and thank you," said Julia warily. She was on the landing and about to go out. "Lovely party."

"Went on for hours. And you took Hussein away, blast you. Still, perhaps it was just as well. Darling, you must be miserable. Why don't you come round and have some coffee and a long good cry."

Everyone wanted her to cry, it seemed. "I'm not in the least miserable, and I've got hundreds of things to do."

"I don't believe it. All doctors in anything but medicine are unemployed these days. What things?"

Julia gave a vague outline.

"My dear! So you're turning litter-rary!" Georgina stretched so that the typewriter sank into the quilt. "But what are you going to live on? Are you sure you're not miserable? I'm marvellous at cheering people up."

"I know you are, bless you. But I'm fine. I've still got a bit of money and I'm living in the present."

"Nonsense. I must get you some reviewing, that'd help a bit." Everyone wanted her to do some reviewing, it seemed. "I'll talk to Desmond Sykes about you." And everyone was going to talk to Desmond Sykes, too.

"Look, it's very sweet of you, Georgina, but I'd rather not. Someone already offered to mention me to Desmond Sykes."

"Who?"

"Marion Farquharson."

"My dear girl, he won't take any notice of what she says. She's a has-been. And completely batty as well."

There was a pause, then Julia's voice was uneasy. "Do you know her?"

"No, only of her. Vaguely. I'm just being bitchy." Julia noticed how in literary circles the admission of a fault was assumed to be equal to its obliteration. "But honestly, darling, I think I'd better see Desmond myself. I can tell him all about you, and the sort of books you'd do best."

"How do you mean, all about me, and what sort of books?"

"Oh, you know, any old thing." Georgina evaded both questions.

"Well, if you like—it's very sweet of you."

"*Niente*. Anything to help a girl in the doldrums. You'll do the same when my turn comes." The future tense sounded imperative.

"Of course. Well, thanks for ringing, and everything."

"Okay. By the way, what have you done with Hussein? I haven't seen him since the party." This was the real point of the call, and Julia sympathised at once. Hussein had been in the British Museum for several days, she told her.

"Oh, well, thanks. And come round when you're miserable. Bye."

Georgina put the receiver down and pondered. Whenever she tried to comfort people, they didn't seem to need it, and she ended up by being miserable herself.

It was half past nine. She had taken her breakfast in bed and had been typing, since eight, a review of a novel translated from the Japanese: *written, unfortunately, with a cunning Oriental eye cocked on Hollywood*, she read, and lit a cigarette. 'To hell with Orientals, to hell with Hussein.' She rattled off the final sentence: *It is, in fact, an exciting scenario, not for a Western, but for an Eastern*. Then her name, and out rolled the page. Georgina shifted the typewriter onto the floor, stretched and finished her cigarette, correcting the typescript.

She had a class at eleven. Slowly she got out of bed and went to the bathroom. She never wore a dressing gown: black silk trousers and a loose printed top did duty as both pyjamas and kimono. Georgina took her time over her toilet and dressing. Although she talked frothily and sailed through her enthusiasms as through so much spray, she was meticulous, both in her studies and in her clothes, a carefully navigated and well-rigged ship. She always managed, with more taste and ingenuity than money, to look too elegant for both University and literary circles. For the former, she combed her hair—not tightly, but so as to leave it soft and wavy in front—into a coiled red snake sitting comfortably on the back of her head; for the latter, she tied it up in a horsetail or wore it loose. Otherwise her personality, in clothes, in speech, and in feeling, remained the same, poised but easy-going, ebullient but reliable.

At twelve o'clock, Georgina came out of her class on *Ki no Tsurayuki*, who had said in 905AD that poetry was helpful as a go-between in love affairs. She made her way to the second floor and knocked on the door of Angela Kriss' room.

"Come in." The voice was sharp, and a male murmur was audible in the background. Through Paul and Hussein, Georgina had come to know Angela well, in fact, rather better than they did, since she was not working under her. But she respected academic achievement, and never forgot she was still a student.

"Hello, professor. I hope I'm not disturbing you." The mixture of politeness and familiarity exactly expressed their relationship.

"Of course you are, Georgina. I'm delighted. Sit down." She switched off a recording machine which was uttering strange masculine sounds. "How are things?"

"Pretty grim. I suppose there's no chance of transferring to African studies? Sanuri, to be precise."

The professor gave her a sharp look. "My dear girl, you're doing your finals in Japanese next year."

"I know. I meant after that. Unless I could change over now."

"Not so easy, you know. Besides, didn't you get a grant as a promising Orientalist?"

"Yes, but—any linguistic training can be reapplied. I've learnt a little already. And they need people in your field."

"Not on Sanuri. One Englishman and a native teaching the language are quite enough. They have one student between them."

"Well, couldn't they do with another?"

"They have enough work as it is," she replied, contradicting herself, and added gently, "take it easy, Georgina."

Georgina sighed and took out a cigarette. "May I?"

"Go ahead."

There was a pause. "He's keeping away," she said at last.

"Isn't that just something we girls have to put up with?" she made a deprecatory gesture. Professor Pekka Nieminen had returned to Helsinki and she didn't feel quite on top of her work either.

"I suppose so. Oh, I knew I'd have to face it sooner or later," Georgina said. "I just thought it would be later, that's all. Do you know whether he's decided to go straight back?"

"Well, there's no point in his staying in England after the end of his contract, this session." Georgina frowned. "He hasn't much money, apart from his salary here." The professor amended her brusqueness with a practical reason.

"I know. Oh, hell. One throws oneself into these things, knowing it won't work, vaguely hoping it might. It's like a fugue with the one theme upside down, contradicting the first. The very knowledge that it can't work is a challenge to break down the barriers. One knows it will end in pain, and at the same time one knows one will get over it."

"One, one, one. Why do we English always use that clumsy, impersonal one when discussing our emotions?" Angel's outburst of grammatical indignation was unduly violent. "You, me, he, it,"—she conjugated in a chant—"that's what matters."

"One wants to be with Hussein." Georgina stuck to the form, but her voice was sad.

"Have you slept with him?" Angela was nothing if not direct.

"No."

"That's a good thing, anyway. You'd never want a white man after that."

"I know." Georgina had learnt more than Japanese in the Far East. "Oh, it wasn't any virtue on my part. And yet"—her voice rose with remembered hopes—"he's so contradictory. You know how his mind runs on proverbs. Sometimes he says two wives are necessary, one to warm

the heart, one to warm the kettle. But then he says the skin creaks according to the country, or again, move your head according to the music."
"So that your skin is creaking and your head is turning."
"That's about it."
"Look, m'dear, I don't want to be brutal, but there are only two things you can do, now, I mean. I take it you've accepted the fact that he won't marry you?"
"I suppose so." Georgina looked wistfully at the map of East Africa on the wall behind Angela's white hair. Large areas were decorated with fluctuating lines and circles, marking, not rivers and hills, but dialect groups, vowel aspirations and glottal stops.
"Of course you have. Apart from anything else, you've got a most promising career here in this building." Georgina shrugged but the professor went on relentlessly. "You must either cut clean, right now—and he is making it easier for you, isn't he?"
"Or?" Georgina ignored the rhetorical question and reminded Angela of her alternative.
"Throw yourself at him shamelessly, have a last fling and get it out of your system."
Georgina was silent. "That wouldn't do, though," she said at last.
"Precisely. The second alternative means more pain for you, the first—probably—more pain for him."
"How?"
"For one thing he would still respect and idealise you. He's very old-fashioned, by our standards, in spite of all those erotic poems."
"Yes." Georgina sighed and got up. There seemed nothing to add. "I'm sorry I bothered you."
"My dear girl. Drop in when you like, you know my timetable. Or at my flat. And one last thing. Don't go confiding in people. You'll feel like hell for a bit, and you'll want to. Keep busy, m'dear, keep busy."
"I'll try. Bless you."
"Goodbye for now."
"Goodbye, professor."
Georgina walked down the corridor, hesitated outside Paul's door and walked on, feeling very firm, though in fact there had been no sound of

voices from inside.

It was nearly one o'clock and she might just catch Desmond Sykes. Ten minutes' walk though Bloomsbury's green squares and dismal streets led her straight into the ramshackle offices of *The Platform*, a weekly so divided against itself and pseudonymously so inbred that it was more generally known as *The Chamber of Deputies*. The main feud, waged quietly but persistently, was between the editor, The Honourable Mrs Robin Trout, who ran the paper as a tattler of moral and intellectual values, and the literary editor, Desmond Sykes, who wanted to Change Things.

"Hello, Desmond. Here's my review of the happy Jap. You free for lunch, by any chance?"

"Hi," said Desmond, so gloomily that it sounded like the last gasp of a dying man. "As it happens, I am free."

In spite of his position, Desmond was by choice a lonely man. Quietly successful and generally respected, he avoided close friendships, preferring to play with numerous acquaintances on a superficial and distinctly physical level. Elderly, bisexual, and a failure in his own eyes, he was anxious to barter reviewing space for other favours from young writers. The latter, however, used him and by-passed him, so that *The Platform*, at his end of it, survived vicariously as a stepping-off ground for continuously changing names, while the main body of the paper continued, solid and unvaried as a company board meeting. Desmond Sykes lived still in the golden age of free expressionism, on which theories of sexual intercourse he became lugubriously eloquent. He wore a pair of halved spectacles, so that when he was not reading he would gaze bleakly upwards over the straight part of the heavy rims, which gave him a sadly surrealistic appearance of having four eyes. It was perhaps his wise acceptance of life which made people misunderstand him, for in fact he was more intelligent than most of the smarter, younger set, and more charitable. In the right mood, and with those who knew him well, he could be extremely good company.

"Oh, dear, I'll have to cut this." Desmond's voice always sounded tragic, even in routine matters.

"That's okay." Georgina was glancing at the books laid out on the table, opening some and putting them back. "You at least cut without a massacre."

"Talking of which"—he was now elegiac—"the BBC are putting on my feature at last. But the fourth dimension and third level of awareness are being cut right out."

"Desmond, I'm delighted." Georgina's enthusiastic tone made up for the ambiguity of her felicitations. "Let's go, shall we? Tell me all about it at lunch. I want to talk to you about a friend of mine."

"Ah," he said sepulchrally. "What sex?"

"Girlfriend."

"Pity. Girls are so morally earnest, these days."

"Nonsense. You bring it out in them. Now do come."

Desmond looked sadly at a galley-proof, sighed and got up. So, yet another name would be creeping into the springboard at the back of *The Platform*, regularly at first, then less and less, until it either slipped away into the morass of nonentity or reappeared on a higher rung, elsewhere.

# Chapter Ten

"THESE damned ah-thrs," said Mr Tweedie, hovering at the door on his way out of Justin Jacob's office. "They seem to think we're berr-sting with £500 advances on unwritten books." He was about fifty, with thick fair hair going white. The mixture of Jewish and Scottish blood gave him business acumen, the courage of a fanciful imagination, and a sharp sense of humour, all indispensable to good publishing.

"Well, I shouldn't worry," said Justin. "If the boy thinks he's a genius just because he's had a few rave reviews, he's in for a slow deflation."

"It's his agent who put him up to this, he'd niverr 'ave thought of it by himself," said Tweedie grumpily. "Och, it's fantastic. I tell ye, young man, the relationship between publisher and agent is like that between the knife and the throat, and I give you one guess as to which is which." He stalked out, leaving Justin to bake in his small top room under the roof, where he was preparing the proofs of Bernard's book on Courtly Love.

The offices of Tweedie and Tweedie hardly matched the smartness of their list. Cold stone stairs led to small landings lined with dusty bookshelves, and posters announcing books published several years before seemed to get older as one climbed further up. The rooms were low and barely furnished, two to each floor. The building typically adapted to the English climate—a refrigerator in winter, a furnace in the one and only heat wave. And the heat wave was happening now, in early June.

Justin had removed the jacket of his well-tailored sea-green barathea suit, and sat in his shirt sleeves—a white nylon shirt almost invisibly specked with blue polka dots, worn open at the neck to show the surprise of a tanned but unhairy chest below the prominent Adam's apple and the darkly Oriental face. He leant back in his chair, with one foot resting nonchalantly on his other knee. His shoes were of a light navy blue suede and his socks were white.

Justin was rather annoyed with Bernard's proofs. The book had been exactly right in typescript, scholarly enough yet lucid and amusing. The problem of the woman's exalted position in Mediaeval Courtly society and its literature had been dealt with simply, with subtly but widely chosen quotations to support the various theories—the social explanation, the Arabic penetration, the classical heritage, the influence of the Catharist heresy. But now the scholarly monster in Bernard had raised its petrifying head. Like serpents everywhere, sentences and footnotes had been inserted throughout the text. No doubt that for Bernard himself, these were only the harmless reflections, thrown from his protective shield, of the real and much more dangerous serpents that would become manifest in the objections and attacks of other scholars. But in the clear, lively print of a Tweedie book they could only turn the reader to stone.

He sighed and turned to Julia Grampion's typed chapter, which had come in that morning. He had read it with pleasure and surprise. The influence of the liturgy on mediaeval religious poetry was hardly a promising subject, yet she had, in under thirty pages, managed to make it light, racy, and highly entertaining. But then so had Bernard with his book, at first. Could scholars then forget themselves only for a moment, only for the private eye of a friendly publisher, donning their clumsy armour as soon as they ventured out into the jousting field? They seemed obsessed with standards, and with what they fondly imagined to be emotional superiority. Afraid of saying too much, they ended by saying too little, cluttering even that with pedantic information. Perhaps his policy had been wrong. But Justin couldn't admit this. 'Women,' he thought hopefully, 'have a lighter touch. And homosexuals. Only a woman or a queer could deal amusingly with Courtly Love.'

He was dining with the Reeves that evening and wondered how he would tackle Bernard. His wife, who was a classicist and a sounder scholar—far too sound for the Tweedie list—always protected him and would defend his additions to the minutest footnote. Justin would have much preferred to see Bernard alone, in a gay restaurant which sparked off his more literary personality.

It was six o'clock, but still very hot. Justin pushed the proofs aside and got up. This was quite enough work for one day and he needed a drink. He picked up the silvery tie which was lying carefully folded in his in-tray and walked over to the mirror hanging on the door. Anxiously he scanned his reflection as he buttoned up his shirt and put on his tie. In spite of the infrared lamp he used at home his face looked as lined as the stretched out hand of a Spanish child, begging, not for coins but for the smooth gold of the Mediterranean sun. He would probably go with Andrew again. Justin sighed and walked back to his chair to put on his sea-green jacket. If only he could forget that damned Negro.

When he got to Russell Square he decided against the pub, and sat outside a small espresso bar near the tube station, sipping an iced coffee. There was just a chance—he looked at his watch. He had twice bumped into Hussein coming from the University, at half past six. Hussein, however, did not come that day.

Disconsolately, Justin went to a pub and and gave himself a double whisky before making his way to Drayton Gardens, in the no-man's land between Kensington and Chelsea, where Bernard had his flat.

Nicolette Reeves, MA (Canterbury), *Docteur ès Lettres*, DLitt, opened the door herself. She was about forty, a little older than Bernard and a little taller. Her dark hair was greying noticeably and she wore it cropped and swept back. Straight black eyebrows almost meeting over an aquiline nose emphasised her French origin, together with an elegant suit of bottle-green grosgrain, cleverly tailored to disguise her thinness.

"Good evening, Justin." Her accent was only traceable in the way she tended to shift the stress to the last syllable, pronouncing his name as if he were "just in" which he was. But she kept to French for her husband's name. "Berr-narr is longing to see you. He is having the usual *craque* before going to print. You must tell him his book is wonderful."

Justin followed her in, filled with foreboding. To his annoyance he saw there was another guest, a woman, who was sitting on the sofa with her back to him.

"Hello, Justin." Bernard got up and greeted him warmly. There was no trace of *craque* on his face and he seemed unexpectedly elated. "I gather you've already met Julia Grampion." Justin recognised her with surprise. She looked plump and pretty in a cool summer frock of white piqué, with black shoes and a black chiffon scarf. Odd wisps of her short hair had been carefully bleached to suggest a scattering of pale autumn leaves, and she had obviously taken advantage of the heat wave to tan her skin. A touch of green eye-shadow changed her blue-grey eyes, which sparkled with a new and witty happiness. 'The effect of writing a specimen chapter,' Justin thought sourly.

"She tells me you're interested in her thesis," Bernard went on. "I examined her on it, and I can tell you it's good." He was unusually hearty. "She's going to do the mediaeval contribution to that book we were discussing, so I thought we'd talk about the whole lot, my book, her book, and our book."

"Hmm." Justin sat down, irritated by this display of tactlessness.

"Berr-narr, give your guest a drink."

"I'm so sorry. What will you have? There's sherry or whisky."

"Whisky, please. Large, if I may, I need it."

"Hard day?"

"Yes. On your damn proofs." Justin decided not to elaborate for the moment. Nicolette had looked up sharply, so he just laughed, and turned to Julia.

"Thank you for sending me the chapter. I've only glanced at it, I'm afraid," he added cautiously, "but it looks fine." This was going to be difficult. Dealing with authors of any kind was complicated enough when one saw them separately. It was complicated enough with an author's wife present. But to be obliged to criticise one author in front of another who had been his student and was to be his collaborator, with the wife thrown in as well and—Justin watched Bernard's eyes on Julia—a possible triangle in the bargain, was a situation most publishers would rather avoid at the end of a tiresome day.

"Well, don't hurry with it," said Julia. She might have been trying to look unconcerned, but she seemed genuinely relaxed even in Nicolette's presence. Perhaps he had been wrong.

"Your belief in the precipitousness of publishers is touching."

She laughed. "I don't expect it's what you want at all. But when is the Courtly Love book coming out? I'm looking forward to that."

Justin noticed that she hadn't said "Bernard's book" and wondered what she called him.

"Well, it's announced for August, but we may have to postpone it." He looked at Bernard steadily. Nicolette was watching him.

"Why?" she asked.

"Oh, various reasons." Justin felt a coward, but he was tired and angry. "You couldn't look in at my office tomorrow some time?"

"Sorry, examinations."

"The cheese soufflé must be just right. Shall we go in to dinner?" Nicolette's instinct for the French art of living as a smoother of situations was exercised with tactful aplomb. Their flat was small, and going in for dinner meant crossing over to the dining alcove in the same room. But Nicolette was meticulous in observances.

"Berr-narr, will you take Julia in?" she gave her arm to Justin. After showing her guests to their places, she disappeared into the kitchen. Bernard opened a bottle of resinated *kokkinelli*, obviously chosen by his wife. He would have preferred Spanish wine himself.

Despite Nicolette's excellent cuisine, the dinner was not a success. Strengthened by food and wine, Justin decided that Bernard's feelings need not be spared, since the situation was of his own making. Gently at first, he suggested cutting out all additions and keeping to the original text. Bernard, on the other hand, had started the evening in a mood of elated irresponsibility and was determined to show no change under the increasing pressure of Justin's attack. He felt protected by the presence of the two women, and justifiably. Nicolette was adamant to the point of sarcasm in defending, not only Bernard, but the integrity of scholarship in the face of popularisation. If publishers wanted to build up a prestige list, she said, they must accept the fact that such books would find only a limited public, and be prepared to lose on them for the cause of learning. "How do you suppose either the public or the University would react if I started popularising my work on early Latin inscriptions?" she demanded, as if Justin had suggested buying up the film rights for them.

Justin replied tartly that Bernard did not for a moment come under the category of their prestige list, that he could have sent his manuscript to one of the University Presses whose vast funds existed precisely to support the cause of true scholarship—he stressed the word 'true'—but that after all Bernard had not in the first place written that kind of book.

The most noticeable change was in Julia. Having light-heartedly accepted Bernard's clumsy pursuit as an agreeable cure for her deep sense of loss, she had been unguiltily delighted to meet his wife, happy and interested to see him in his home context. At first she had kept quiet. But as her trust in his literary abilities waned with an increasing sympathy for Justin's point of view, so her irritation with Nicolette's archness mounted, bristling up the feeling of anxiety which had been so easily smoothed over with Bernard's tenderness, his gaiety and their mutual interests. Because of this, she found herself supporting Nicolette's defence of Bernard, without realising that by doing so she was spoiling her own chances in Justin's estimation. She was, in fact, treating them as one: by supporting Nicolette she was defending Bernard, though more gently. Yet all the time she was aware that had the argument been between the couple she would have sided, also more gently, with Nicolette against him. She preferred not to find out whether such hypothetical behaviour would be motivated by guilt for encouraging his deception, or by a desire to disguise her own growing protective instincts.

Justin himself became calmer as he grew inwardly more furious. With three scholars ranged against him he was far more sure of himself as a publisher than if one of them had unexpectedly helped him out. But apart from knowing that he was right, he had soon grasped the situation and now felt justifiably annoyed at having been used as a mere opportunity for Bernard to introduce a girlfriend, plausibly, to his wife. Justin cursed the English inability to keep these things separate, the hypocritical desire to make it social, innocent-looking and cosy. The very friendliness had a kick in it for them, giving rise to pleasing little situations of *double-entendre*. He was watching Nicolette, who, he knew, was no fool.

"Well," he said, when they were sitting more quietly over coffee, "it's your book, after all, and only our imprint." He had kept the trump card to the last. "But we may have to stick to the letter of the contract and charge you for excess alternations in the proofs. Half the pages have to be reset and the printer's bill will be enormous." There was a pause. "Anyway, I'll talk to Tweedie about it tomorrow and let you know."

"All right. I'm sure we can come to some sort of—er—agreement." Bernard was not going to compromise except privately. The conversation turned to other topics with astonishing rapidity. Bernard started a eulogy of London University. One isn't just a don there, he said, one is a Londoner as well. One meets other people far more often than one meets one's colleagues. Nicolette, who had always longed for a Girton fellowship, in a really English university, disagreed violently. Too many distractions. But that's life, said Bernard with a capital L in his voice. Julia said that this was all very well if one had friends in London anyway: the University's own social life was a pretty dreary affair. Justin, who had been to St Andrews, made it clear that he thought poorly of English education. Neither Julia's book nor the symposium on adultery was discussed, and after a suitable interval Justin took his leave.

"How about you, Julia? Can I see you safely home?"

She hesitated, aware of the opportunity for bettering her own prospects by making peace, but afraid that Bernard and Nicolette might guess her motives. Justin certainly did and smiled. He rather liked her transparence.

"It's very kind of you, but I think I'll stay a little while—if I may," she turned to Nicolette and added gauchely, "I want to discuss the other book with Bernard."

When Justin got out he walked angrily to South Kensington station. "These damned authors," he echoed Tweedie's words, "perhaps after all there is something to be said for dealing with them through agents." The night was warm and he longed more than ever for his holiday. Spain, Italy, anywhere, with anyone, alone, even with that tedious boy Andrew.

As he got out of the train at Leicester Square to change for the Northern Line, an extraordinary sight greeted his eyes. A dark figure in a yellow turban, wearing a European shirt, a brown stole wrapped around it and a long, bright blue open skirt over his trousers, loomed high above the crowd. It was Hussein. He must have been on the same train.

Justin blushed even in the cadaverous neon lighting of the underground. Hussein saw him and greeted him with the usual flash of white teeth that electrocuted Justin from the waist down.

"I have been to a party," he said as they walked towards the escalator, "with many of my countrymen. All dressed." He pointed proudly to his clothes.

"What was it, a national feast?"

"No. Doctor Borrodick, you know him? At the University." Justin shook his head. "Paul Borrodick, I work with him," Hussein insisted, as if London were an African village. "He gave a farewell party for me. We sang much po-ettery."

"Farewell?" Justin's heart thumbed wildly as they stepped onto the escalator, which counterpointed its rhythm under his feet.

"One about the elephant—O ugly father, old cow of Kusi Bayo," Hussein improvised a translation, "stupid one with longs ears, you stumble and roar like the autumn sky. It is beautiful?"

"Yes." Justine had decided against the Northern Line. "When do you go?"

"Tomorrow." Hussein was staring at the numerous advertisements for uplift which lined the walls of this modern ascent from Avernus. "Here is another—O you with your drooping breasts that wander to your knees, give yourself to me. Your eyes are shields, back with white shield-cloths. O my love which burns like fire, which comes like colic. You like this one?"

Justin was standing on the step above, going backwards to listen to him, so that his eyes were level with the yellow turban. "Hussein," he said urgently, "I want to hear more. Will you come home with me, tonight?" he half stepped down and pressed his body against Hussein's, putting his hand on his shoulder. But at this moment they reached the top and he had to turn and jump off.

Hussein had at last understood. His face was rigid and his body erect as they walked past the ticket collector and up the stairs. They came out into the street and stopped. Justin was looking agonised as well as hot, and he panted a little as he breathed the cooler air, though the night was sultry. Hussein looked down at him and his eyes filled with compassion. "Mister Jacob, I am sorry. I cannot."

"I know." Justin was already regretting his reckless move.

"They gave it to him and it did not fill the ring of the thumb and forefinger," Hussein announced to the closed bookshops of the Charing Cross Road. "They took it away and it seemed to fill the whole plain."

Justin looked sad and bewildered. "Goodbye, Hussein. Good luck." He put out his hand.

Hussein shook it solemnly, bowed and smiled. "Goodbye, Mister Jacob." And as Justin turned to dive back into the mouth of Hades, Hussein called out after him, "pray to your angel, Mister Jacob, pray to your angel."

# Chapter Eleven

"JOJINA." Hussein stood at the door of her flat an hour later. "I have come to say goodbye."
Georgina stood in her black and flowered silk pyjamas, her red hair tumbling round her shoulders. She was familiar with his national dress, but his sudden colourful appearance so late at night startled her. She had not seen him since her party, nearly a month before.
"Hussein," she whispered. Her face went as white as his shirt, and her blue eyes were wide and frightened. "When are you leaving?"
"Tomorrow, on the boat, at night. When He has sown His chick-peas in the sky." They still stood in the doorway. He stretched out his hand to touch her hair and she stepped back a little. His hand dropped. "I walked in the street so long. The eyes have no axe to cut mountains, the mind has no ships." Georgina waited, undecided and anguished. "Since the beggar would come anyway, it's best to invite him first," said Hussein.
"Come in a moment," she said at last. She was trembling.
"You are the red star, the one which shines brightest." He followed her in.
"Venus?"
"Yes. We call her Kabalcha."
They sat down, rather formally, on two red cushions. He gazed at her white throat, slowly removing his turban.
Georgina looked alarmed. "Hussein, you mustn't stay long."
He smiled. "I have composed a poem for you. It goes in English like this: *Between five red cushions, between four walls, I sit on the ground. Between five plates, between two cups, I have eaten and I am hungry. I have stretched and I have not slept. I am dead.*"
"Why five?" Georgina interrupted, so as not to show her emotion.
"*I am broken like the horn of a goat*," Hussein pursued. "*My hands are stronger than yours, they have cut down the castor tree. My feet are stronger*

than yours, they will reach Sanuri. My eyes are stronger than yours, they follow the vulture flying. My heart is not so strong as yours, it breaks like a pumpkin. Love strikes men like a stick. O Jojina, how long shall I meet you with my eyes. A javelin without blood is not a javelin. Love without kisses is not love." He leant towards her and plunged his hand into the fire of her red hair at the back of her neck. "Come, we will suck each other as the calf sucks the breast. Jojina, your teeth are the first fruits."

"Hussein, no, no." Georgina's voice was desperate. "Please. It will only make it worse. You're going away."

He was gentle, fondling her hair, his black fingers with their white nails tracing her features. He bent over her, his teeth bit softly into her lower lip and his hand swept under loose pyjama top, scooping her breasts, pressing her ribs, darkly embroidering the small of her back. He smelt, not of earth but of continents. She gasped, and he slipped his other arm under knees, lifted her tenderly as he got up and carried her into the next room. The quilted bed, from which she had risen to open the door, was expecting them.

It was three in the morning when Georgina lay weeping quietly on Hussein's smooth black shoulder, her hair spread over his chest like red seaweed on a rock, her white arm flung across him like a rope. He was staring at the wooden ceiling.

"Jojina," he murmured, "do not cry." She gave a loud sob which shook her body, and he pressed his arm more tightly around it. "I will tell the ship to go without Hussein. I will stay here with you."

"You know you can't do that."

"If I go back, I would be like the bustard, who has seen an enemy, and cannot sleep. I would be a lioness, whose young cubs have been killed, I would make much clamour. My tribe will divided against itself. I am angry at it."

Georgina held her breath. "And Allah?"

Hussein still stared at the ceiling. There was a long silence. "*Qarsa malqau Qawayu*," he murmured. "Old god, decrepit old god," he intoned, "listen. You have ears as old as the mountains, listen. You have eyes like the sea, look at us. You have hands like the scorched plain, take all the camels. You love beautiful black women, take them. Leave me with

Jojina, who is white as an elephant's tusk."

Georgina was frightened by this strange prayer. Why had he started it in Sanuri and then translated? Was its power diminished for him, in English? Surely if he had meant it he would have said it in his own language? She did not know that it was a pagan prayer, not addressed to Allah.

She slept at last. Hussein lay awake for a long time, not moving his arm from under her head, and still staring at the ceiling.

They had breakfast formally, Japanese-fashion, sitting opposite each other on two cushions with the little low table between them. Georgina's face was white and drawn, but her eyes were deeply still as mountain lakes.

"I will go to the ship and tell him to sail away."

"In our country," said Georgina, "a ship is female." She was feeling much calmer, happy in his presence, and prepared even to bring him to his senses. "You mustn't do anything rash, Hussein. Why don't you go home first, and then see. If you can't forget me, you will come back."

"Maybe the European will go far away, maybe the stars will change," said Hussein sadly. "I go to the ship and tell him to sail."

Georgina's sigh started as a sad sigh and ended in deep content. But she knew herself well. Now she felt she could do without him. Now was the time to urge his caution. Tomorrow, tonight even, she would want him again. It would be bad enough, for long enough, as things stood, but she knew it would be worse if he stayed, because in the end, he would still go back. Family pressure would be too great, and the practical difficulties of living in England would not be overcome, even if she supported him. At the most, they would have three months.

"Look, Hussein, why don't you go and talk to Paul first. Your ship doesn't sail till tonight," she paused and added gently, "he might be able to suggest some way you could earn money if you stay."

Hussein looked doubtful. "Perhaps, yes. But I go to the ship after and tell him to sail."

When he had gone, Georgina leant against the door for a moment. Then she walked slowly towards the partition, picking up a cigarette and her lighter on the way, and went into the other room. She lay down on the unmade bed, leaning against the wall and smoking. After a few minutes, she stubbed out the cigarette and picked up the telephone. It was ten to nine.


Julia had got into the habit of lingering over breakfast and starting her day in the Reading Room at ten, so that she was not quite dressed when her doorbell rang. Puzzled, she put on her dressing gown and went down. It was Paul. A taxi was just driving off.

"Julia, I need your help. It's about Hussein. It's urgent. Can I come up a minute?"

"Yes, of course."

He needed her help. But only for someone else. They went upstairs in silence. Her first reaction on seeing him had been one of shock, draining the blood from her face, but followed at once by annoyance, which sent it rushing back. Now she felt the same pounding of her heart as on their previous meeting under the columns, and the little beads of cold sweat came out again on her brow. Yet she had stopped missing him, thinking of him only at intervals, neither with anger nor with longing. She knew now how a man could feel, flooded with the realisation of love only on seeing the woman. The process of rooting out was exactly the same in both, it merely took a woman a longer time, unless given strength from outside. She had been given a man's emotional independence, artificially, by filling herself with another man's emotions, about which she cared little. They went into her room.

"Shall I warm up some coffee?" her breakfast things were still out.

"I can only stay a minute. But yes, that would be nice." He sat down at the table and surveyed the once familiar room. Nothing had changed. He noticed that she still threw out her pillow at night. He gazed at her sadly as she bent over the gas ring. "I came by taxi from Earls Court," he said, to break the awkwardness.

"What's up?" she got out an extra cup and put it on the table.

"Georgina rang me up this morning. You know Hussein is catching the boat tonight." She nodded. "Well, apparently he called on her after my party last night to say goodbye. I couldn't make out whether he stayed with her or not, and naturally didn't press it, but whatever happened, he's decided to cancel and stay in England."

"Well," said Julia slowly, "why not?"

"Look, I can't go into all that. You know as well as I do why not. Georgina knows, too. She was in great distress." Julia poured out the coffee and handed him his cup in silence. Paul's tone softened. "She says she can't take any more, she'd rather he went now than later. And he's bound to go back, whatever happens."

"I suppose you're right."

"I know I am. Don't you remember Gulenne, who stayed in Europe for that German girl? He had to cut himself off completely, give up his religion and all his ties. He was working in the docks and still is. But Hussein's different."

There was a pause. "What do you want me to do?"

"Georgina said she told him to come and see me first, so I must be in my room all day. But it's quite possible he won't." He sipped his coffee and noticed that she still curled her hair round her fingers when nervous. "I've already rung up the shipping office and asked them to telephone me if he comes in, and put him on the line. But it's very difficult for me." He took out his cigarettes and offered her one. She shook her head, making no comment on his smoking before lunch as he lit up his own. "Sanuris are proud and sensitive, and Hussein may think I want him to go, personally, or that I won't help him to get work."

"Surely not?"

"Well, he might. You know him well and he trusts you. There would be no possible ulterior motive in you. Could you go round to his digs and talk to him, if he's there?"

"I don't see why he should be."

"He's bound to go there sometime today."

"It's asking rather a lot. I can't hang around the East End inquiring for a coloured man all day."

"Darling, I don't want you to hang around." The word slipped out naturally, but its unexpectedness troubled her. She looked at him and tears filled her eyes. But she didn't cry. He was embarrassed, then smiled and took her hand. "I'm sorry. I meant, could you call there, and if he's out, leave a message telling him you want to say goodbye. Ask him to meet you somewhere, and if he doesn't call once again this afternoon. You can't do more. We none of us can."

"No, we can't. After all, it's not really our business." But she had made up her mind. "The trouble is, I've already said goodbye. He came to the Reading Room yesterday."

"Well, say you have an urgent message from me, or from Georgina, say she's gone away. Anything."

"All right."

"Bless you, darling." He got up and kissed her on the forehead. His thin beard touched her cheek and she turned aside, putting her face in her hands. But he lifted it and kissed her again, very lightly, on the lips. There was a knock on the door and the landlady came in.

"Well, if it isn't Mr Brodrick!" she exclaimed. She took in the unmade bed, Julia's dressing gown and the two coffee cups at a glance. "Well," she repeated, "isn't that luv'ly? It's ever so nice to see you back. I always says to Miss Julia, I says, she was too strict with you, sending you out like that, ever so good like, every night."

Paul looked at Julia and smiled, shrugging his shoulders and raising his eyebrows to forestall useless argument.

"You're very kind, Mrs Moffat," he said. "I have to rush now, I'm afraid. Julia," he turned to her and spoke in a low voice. Mrs Moffat watched them, leaning on her mop so that her blue hair looked like the wrong end of it. "Are you sure you believe in what I'm asking you to do? No doubts or regrets?"

"No, I'm not sure. You know how I feel about these taboos. But I'll do it, don't worry." Her voice was barely audible, even to Mrs Moffat, straining though she was to hear.

"Bless you again. Goodbye." He didn't kiss her this time and walked to the door.

"Regrets indeed!" said Mrs Moffat. "I should think not! What a nice couple you always was. It weren't right, Mr Brodrick, leavin' 'er like that, it weren't right, that's what I says. Proper miserable she was."

Paul smiled at her, then at Julia, specially, with his blue eyes narrowed, and went out.

## Chapter Twelve

"WHAT ever happened to you? I thought you were never coming?" Bernard leant over Julia. She sat sorting out her tickets at one of the narrow middle tables between the rows of the Reading Room. It was half past twelve and her usual seat was taken. Most people avoided these tables, they were so uncomfortable, and the readers sitting there were usually late-comers. Out of the corner of her eye, Julia had seen Bernard look up as she walked past his row, but she hadn't stopped. He had followed her while she looked for somewhere to sit and now his voice was anxious.

"Oh, I got caught up in various things." She was purposely vague, then felt sorry for him. He must have thought she was avoiding him. "Anyway, you said last night you'd be examining all day."

"Did I? Oh, yes, to Justin. That was only an excuse not to go to his office. He was trying to stall and see me alone, and I wanted to settle it there and then."

"Could you be quiet, please," snapped a woman in a blowsy mauve dress.

"You free for lunch?" Bernard whispered without bothering to apologise to the woman.

"Yes. I'll just put my tickets in."

The heat wave was still on and Julia was wearing the same white dress, this time with green sandals and a green choker necklace. But white in London, like newly washed windows, didn't last more than a day, and the piqué was no longer quite so crisp. Bernard, however, who had gone bohemian, unfashionable, in a maroon shirt and brown corduroy trousers, noticed only the general effect, measuring her plump figure with the hunger in his eyes.

"I shall have to get back by half past one," said Julia as they went down the steps. "Someone may be looking for me here this afternoon."

"Oh?"

"Hussein. He's leaving tonight and I have an urgent message for him."

"You're a strange girl." Bernard decided that he hated Hussein, and felt irrelevantly pro-Apartheid. "Philologists, mediaevalists, Negroes. You're doing fine."

"Oh, come off it." Julia echoed almost his first words to her, absently. She was worried. Hussein had not been seen at his digs since the previous afternoon. Moreover, she had been upset by Paul's visit.

Bernard changed his tactics. "Darling, I was only teasing. You look so stunning in that dress, I can't bear anyone else even talking to you." She said nothing. She liked him to be jealous, but she had always been annoyed by the premature and proprietary way he called her 'darling', almost from the first. She reserved the word for intimacy, which she had no intention of allowing. Her silence increased his uncertainty.

"I want to talk to you," he said, taking her arm as they crossed the road, "about those wretched proofs. I had a hell of a row with Nicolette after you'd gone last night."

This time he hit the mark. There was nothing in the world like domestic difficulties for rousing a woman's protective instinct, especially over a subject on which she was, or felt, more expert than the wife. "Let's go somewhere nice," she said affectionately, "I can't face the smell and clatter of Lyons' today."

They went to a dark Italian place, decorated with mock vine-trellising and Chianti bottles, and blissfully cooled by two large electric fans. Bernard perked up as he showed off his not very good Italian, ordering *spaghetti alla bolognese* and *biff di vitella con insalata*. In a fit of heat and exhibitionism he undid two more shirt buttons, revealing an unexpected forest of hair, much darker than his fairness would suggest. Julia was startled into an easily resistible impulse to plunge her hand in it. She didn't resist it and playfully poked one finger down his shirt across the small table, when no waiter was near.

He became very tender and serious and started talking about his marriage. Since his first curious offer of himself as a cushion, he had steered a careful course between gaiety and affection, sincere enough in his desire merely to cheer her up. If he had seen and quickly used the oppor-

*The Languages of Love: Chapter Twelve*

tunity of her distress to make room for himself, she for her part was half consciously drifting into the sympathetic role he had assumed at the beginning. She knew that he was using her just as he had told her to use him. But it seemed a fair enough exchange, for the time being at least. She basked in the obvious attraction he felt for her; and their minds, on a certain level, clicked and fitted like two dented wheels inside a clock. Sooner or later, the clock would stop, with no harm done and no need to wind it up again.

When they got around to the question of the proofs, Julia veered to Justin's point of view, urging Bernard to compromise or, better still, to let the original text appear untouched.

"After all, Courtly Love is a potential seller, whether you like it or not. How can it compare with Latin inscriptions? It touches everyone, we have the relics of it in popular songs and in Hollywood films. They're the modern equivalent of your romances and troubadour lyrics."

Bernard looked a little put out. "Well, I didn't popularise to that extent, you know, even in the first version."

"Of course you didn't," she said soothingly. "I'm sure it's a very scholarly book. I only meant that you shouldn't clutter up a very human subject with footnotes. Justin said the original version was exactly what they wanted, sound but entertaining, and delicately treated."

"Why didn't you say all this yesterday?"

Julia hesitated. "It's difficult to explain. I wanted to, but I felt peculiarly impelled to support Nicolette. For one thing it was a way of defending you against Justin. He did become rather sardonic. And, well"—she looked at him shyly—"Nicolette's way of defending you was so, how shall I put it, severe, it seemed to squash you out of academic existence. I wanted to tone it down."

"Oh, darling." He took her hand.

"And then, somehow, I thought you'd come round to Justin's views on your own, which is always better." She gave him a wicked smile. "One usually ends up by turning against one's supporters, especially when they're vehement." The waiter brought their coffee.

"You're more subtle than I thought," said Bernard with something close to adoration in his eyes. He noticed suddenly that she wasn't wearing her crucifix.

"If I were really subtle I wouldn't explain it all." But she smiled, feeling wise and protective. "I'm Aquarius, and have a morbid passion for dotting all the *is*."

"Like Nicolette. But much more charmingly. She's French and very rational."

"I know. I rather took to her, at first."

"So did I." He smiled wryly. "She's a marvellous wife, of course, and always stimulating."

Julia reverted to their own subject. "Seriously, Bernard, you don't need to be afraid of over-popularising. Just have the courage to remove the claptrap."

"But some of it is necessary. The hermetic love-language of the *trobar clus*, in Provençal, for example, is a controversial topic. I can't simply choose one interpretation without a footnote to show there are others." She gazed at him wonderingly, troubled by his strange interests. "I adore the way you curl your hair round your fingers when you concentrate," he added.

She stopped doing it. "Cut it down to a minimum. You should produce a book which will interest all kinds of people, scholars and laymen alike. We all suffer from the dregs of Romantic Love. It's highly artificial and unhealthy."

"Is it?" he looked at her intensely. "I'm an incurable romantic, really."

"So am I." She thought of Paul and her own irrational conviction that nothing should interfere with the course of true love. She thought of Georgina and Hussein. Then she remembered. "Heavens, I must get back. It's nearly two."

Bernard had misunderstood her reply and took her arm as they went out, running his hand up almost into her armpit. She shuddered, responding more violently than she had thought possible.

It was hot even in the Reading Room and she found it impossible to work. So did Bernard. He became quite adolescent, walking past her desk and depositing amorous little notes in reconstructed Indo-European, in Gothic, in Middle English, in Provençal. She examined his split-up, pointed handwriting, noting the uncertainty beneath the self-assurance, and

## The Languages of Love: Chapter Twelve

the basic confidence beneath the uncertainty; but noting especially his flagrant sensuality. The lonely Pole who had made so many *Approaches* to Dostoievski renewed his approaches to her and the lecherous Indian was on the prowl again. A man in spectacles threw a rubber deftly under her chair, disturbed her to pick it up, and asked her if he had not met her in Oxford. She began to feel like a bitch on heat.

Hussein didn't turn up. Julia was more and more of the opinion that it was none of her business. By five o'clock, the last thing she wanted to do was to trail to the East End again and look for him.

Bernard was waiting for her as usual in the hall and held her bare arm close to him as they walked towards the railings where his Lambretta was parked. "I want to take you for a long, long ride. And then make love to you for hours in a deserted field."

The sun was beating down on them. Julia looked at his firm thick lips and felt hers parting in a sudden surge of desire. She made up her mind on the spur of that desire. "Why don't you come and have tea at my place?"

They climbed aboard and bruited off. He swerved recklessly into Gower Street, with her arms pressed round his open-shirted torso and her head leaning on his back.


She lay half undressed on the bed, comforting him. "Never mind, darling. It doesn't matter."

He was sobbing, without tears. "But it does. It's just—oh, I've wanted you for so long. I was frightened of you, that you'd find me middle-aged and inadequate. And I am."

"Shh. Don't get upset. Oh, darling, darling."

"You've never called me that before."

"I know. I didn't mean it before."

"I wanted it to be so perfect."

"It will be," she said gently, stroking his hair. She had been inwardly furious at first, but now she was calm and filled with a strange tenderness. She wanted to take him in hand, to restore his confidence, to make him truly hers.

There was a knock on the door, which was locked. She leapt up, rushed to the cupboard and snatched her dressing gown. Bernard started dressing hurriedly. Signing to him to keep silent, she turned the key in the lock and opened the door a fraction, expecting to tell Mrs Moffat that she was resting. It was Paul. Julia was visibly terrified. He obviously expected to be asked in.

"I—I was asleep," she stammered.

"Mrs Moffat let me in. Did you find Hussein?"

"Well, no." She suddenly spoke very fast, still holding the door ajar. "He wasn't there this morning and hadn't been since yesterday." Paul nodded impatiently as if he knew this already. "I left an urgent message that he was to come to the British Museum, but he didn't."

"He hasn't been to the shipping office, either, and they know nothing of his cancellation. He didn't come to see me."

"Maybe he's decided to go after all."

"I doubt it. He would have gone back to his digs to pack his things by now. He hasn't, I rang them up. You didn't try again at five." He looked at her reproachfully.

"No."

"Can't I come in?"

"Well, I'd rather not." There was a creak from the bed as Bernard overbalanced on his hand while trying to tidy the counterpane.

"I see." Paul's face went white with anger. He spoke with an effort. "I'll go to his digs now. But I think he simply decided not to sail, without letting them know."

"Try ringing Georgina." Julia's voice was dead.

"I have. She hasn't seen him either. He seems to have disappeared."

"He's bound to turn up."

"Well, thank you for what you did." The words were succinct with sarcasm. He turned his face away and said, "goodbye. I'm sorry I—er—woke you up."

## Chapter Thirteen

THE stall-holders of Berwick Market in Soho were shouting to each other in Cockney, in Italian, in expletives, as they unloaded large sacks of new potatoes, cabbages, cauliflowers, carrots, Jerusalem artichokes and podded peas from numerous lorries which blocked the narrow street. Cases of oranges, of Grannysmiths as green as dawn and Jonathans as red as sunset, baskets of strawberries from Kent, of blackberries, red cherries, big melons and pineapples, boxes of lettuces, tomatoes or shining purple aubergines, of green corn or seakale, and packets of dark steaming beetroot, were being passed quickly from hand to hand, finding their places as if by a disciplined regimentation on the lined up stalls and barrows. It was seven o'clock in the morning.

The delicatessen shops and the cafés were still closed and few of Soho's inhabitants were up. From a private door at the side of a dubious-looking chemist a man stumbled out, scowling at the continuance of life outside. A blonde hurried by, in high heels and black nylons, with a yellow gabardine thrown carelessly over her shoulders, revealing, as she walked, a brief gold *frou-frou* of the kind worn by cabaret dancers or cigarette girls. Two policeman stood nonchalantly near a hairdresser's shop, hiding its photographic display of wavy styles temptingly offered to the Edwardian gentlemen of Soho.

"Cor blimey! Look what's coming 'ere!" A man on a lorry dropped the sack of potatoes he had just lifted. Shouts were heard from stalls further down and the alleyway between them was suddenly flooded with people, fat women wearing aprons of sackcloth, small dark men in shirt sleeves, all deserting their urgent work to yell and gesticulate at the spectacle, unusual even for Soho, which now greeted their vegetable-dazed eyes. The man on the lorry took off his cap and scratched his black curls. "Cor strike me dreaming. Western Desert an' all."

A black-faced figure in a yellow turban was advancing, head high above the crowd, wearing a white shirt, a brown stole twisted round it and a long blue cotton skirt over his trousers. Behind him, led on a short thin rope, a baby camel ambled majestically, laden with rich colourful raiments and casting scornfully sleepy eyes over the shouting men and women, the packing-cases, and the paralysis of motorised transport.

Hussein had purposely chosen an early hour to avoid onlookers, for he was discreet by disposition, but he had not reckoned with the market, or with Soho's continental habits. Windows began to open, shop-grills were lifted with much grinding and clanging, shutters were slammed outwards. And more: the people were clustering in front of him, frightened of the animal which might kick, bite or spit, but determined not to let him go through without some explanation for this exotic disturbance of their morning routine.

The two policemen made their way imperturbably through the crowd. "Now, now," said the taller one, taking out his notebook, "what's this all about?"

"He is Gedo." Hussein stroked the camel's nose affectionately. The other policeman politely tried to take the rope from his hand, but Hussein held on to it firmly. "He is for Jojina. My wedding perr-sent."

The tall policeman looked up at him, bewildered. If at first he had thought this was an eccentric character escaped from a circus, he now began to fear that he was dealing with that foreign prince who was continually marrying famous film stars, or worse still, with one of those important political figures the press were always fussing about. Perhaps it was the Kabaka. Or had the Kabaka gone home? "I'm very sorry, sir"—he touched his helmet cautiously—"but I shall have to ask you a few questions. Nothing to worry about, sir, all in the line of duty."

"Certainly," said Hussein grandly and beamed at him. "You wish to know the customs of my country?"

The other policeman began to press the crowd back, expertly. "Now move along there please. Get back to your work now. Make room there please." A small circular space was formed around the group, but the crowd remained, shouting and laughing.

The tall policeman was taking notes. "What is your name, sir?"

"Hussein Mekahil Abdillahi."

"I beg your pardon?"
Hussein offered to write it down, still holding on to the rope.
"Domicile?"
"I do not understand."
"Where do you live—sir?" The policeman was disappointed that Hussein was not the Kabaka, but he remained polite, out of habit and just in case.
"There." Hussein pointed vaguely westwards. "From today."
"The address?"
He gave Georgina's address.
"And your previous address?"
He gave that too. "And before that I lived in Sanuri."
"Do you have an address there, sir?"
Hussein was silent and shook his head.
"Have you any papers? A passport?"
"I have, but not here."
"Well now, sir. Can you tell me where you got this camel?"
"Gedo. He is only a foal and I have only one, it is very sad. In my country we give many camels. One to the mother and a hundred to the father, and a bay pony to the brother. But Jojina is alone and here I am not rich."
"But where did you get it?"
"From the ship. He was for the Zoo, he was a perr-sent."
The policeman looked puzzled.
"A perr-sent for the Zoo, from a sultan. I do not know which sultan."
"But how did you get hold of it?" The voice sounded more suspicious, and "sir" was dropped.
Hussein flashed his teeth happily. "I went to the Zoo, yesterday. I talked with the director of the Zoo and he said that the Zoo had many camels and foals, too. So I bought him. Gedo." He rubbed noses with the camel.
"Well, thank you, sir." The policeman had enough to go by in his notebook. "We'll have to check up on that, I'm afraid."
Hussein nodded. "A lie can be overtaken," he said simply. "A truth stays still."
The two policemen looked at each other.

"Fortune has not grown old and law is everlasting. God is all-knowing and the high-born have the news."

"I beg your pardon?"

"It is a proverb. Sanuris may tell lies, but we do not make false proverbs. Can I go to Jojina now? I am late."

There was a shout from one of the bystanders. The camel had turned his head and was nibbling at the artificial green thatch on one of the stalls. " 'Ey, you leave me roof alone!" A short fat man in a vest stepped forward and gesticulated to the camel, not daring to touch it.

"It'll make 'im sick!" The crowd was laughing and chattering. " 'Ere, 'ave you ever seen a camel bein' sick?"

Touched by the English concern for his animal, Hussein tugged at the rope and bowed all round, smiling.

"You can't go through the London streets with a camel, I'm afraid," said the constable. "It's creating a disturbance. The traffic's just beginning."

"But I must. It is for Jojina. We are getting married." Hussein was firm.

"Where are you going?"

"Just there. Warwick Street."

The policemen didn't know what to do. To take Hussein and his camel to the police station would be as disturbing as to let him go round the corner. They muttered together for a moment. Then the shorter of them departed to report the incident and ask for instructions. The other turned to Hussein. "I'll accompany you," he said. "To protect you."

Hussein bowed again.

"Now move along there. Make way please." The crowd moved back to let the short procession through. The stall-holders went regretfully back to their work, but many more people had by now gathered and most of them followed behind the camel, shouting excitedly. During the interrogation, a smart barrow-boy had slipped away to ring up several newspapers, giving his name to each in the hope of payment for information. Two press-cars and a taxi drew up simultaneously in Shaftesbury Avenue, coughing up three reporters and two camera men. They raced up Rupert Street and were quickly directed to the vanishing cortège.

Georgina was woken up by the downstairs bell being pressed urgently five times, followed by several loud thumps of the knocker. The commotion in the street was alarming, and several windows screeched up. She leapt out of bed and peered through the printed curtains. With a gasp of astonishment, in which mingled both terror and relief, she raced downstairs.

There were murmurs of excitement among the crowd when she appeared on the doorstep, her tousled red hair falling over the Japanese flowered smock that topped her black silk trousers. Her feet were bare and very white. "Hussein!"

A camera bulb flashed.

"Jojina. You are an ostrich standing in the morning, shaking her wings. Jojina, I buy your love with a camel. Only one camel, it is very sad, he is so small. But he will grow. He brings you many cloths in many colours. He is all I have." He unstrapped the silk raiments, unfolded each one for her admiration and piled them one by one on her arms. The crowd cooed with each colourful display.

"What is his name?"

"Gedo."

Georgina was dazed into complete acceptance of her strange situation. She also knew that she must not argue now. Her calm hypnotised the crowd into a hushed silence, so that their voices, though quiet, were heard clearly.

"Gedo." She advanced towards him, still holding her silken burden. "I like him, Hussein. Thank you. Where is he going to live?"

"I have not thought."

She saw the policeman standing behind the camel. Several more policemen had arrived to hold the people back and more photographers were pushing their way forward.

"The warehouse opposite," she said quickly, "I think it's empty. I'll ask if I can use it for the time being. What does a camel eat, Hussein?"

"Saltbush. But then he needs more water. He likes the leaves of the damag-tree and the olive and the acacia," he elaborated, impractically.

Georgina smiled. "We'll find him something."

"He will not drink for a long time," Hussein reassured her. "I asked them on the ship. The gave him much and he keeps it in there." He pointed to the hump.

"Wait." She ran upstairs to dress, taking the coloured silks. It was not till nearly noon that the baby camel was finally installed in the small warehouse opposite Georgina's flat. The original crowd had dispersed but was constantly replenished by newcomers, the story being handed down the hourly generations by word of mouth, like a minor epic. By then a newsreel man had arrived and was quietly filming the whole scene from the top of his car, well behind the crowd. A police officer had turned up to ask more questions and was satisfied that the animal would now be treated as a private pet, rather than as a public nuisance.

At twelve o'clock Georgina, who had organised everything and everyone with tense aplomb, began to feel the strain. In the middle of answering a reporter's question, she pulled Hussein into the house, nimbly stepped back and shut the door, suddenly ready for the reaction rising in her throat, of tears, entreaties, and despair.

## Chapter Fourteen

"I LIKED you from the start, my dear, and I'm absolutely delighted." Marion Farquharson sat back in Julia's armchair, stirring her tea and looking round the room. Hrothgar and Wiglaf were busy with dressing-up games under the table, where they had withdrawn with various items Julia had lent them from her wardrobe.

"Look," said Wiglaf, emerging draped in her green poplin skirt and waving the poker, "I'm Merlin."

Marion had enclosed a note in Professor Jarvis-Anderson's congratulatory letter. She would be coming to town to buy shoes for the two elder boys, it said, and unless she heard by telephone that it wasn't convenient, she would call at Gower Street for tea.

"You're very kind," said Julia, offering her a piece of cake. "It's funny, I had almost forgotten about the job. So much seems to have happened since I had the interview."

"Ah, the camel, you mean?" Marion smiled at the cream which oozed out of her cake and tackled it with a happy disregard for her ample figure.

"That too."

Marion looked up sharply, then took another mouthful while she considered the possibilities of that remark. She decided to ignore it. "How on earth did *you* get involved in all that? I saw your name in the papers."

"I know. I've had three reporters here already, wanting a different angle on the story—Hussein's life history, how well did I know him, had I tried to prevent it, etc. I suppose they must have got on to the Afro-Asian Department and bothered Paul."

"Paul?"

"Paul Brodrick. Hussein was working with him. He used to be—well, we were engaged at one time, and he asked me to help him find Hussein on Tuesday. He must have told them."

"I see."

"Grrr. Whoosh. I'm a dragon." Hrothgar crawled up, his legs lost in Julia's leopard-skin slacks, which she had bought in a rash fit of optimism about her plumpness and never worn. His front and head were wrapped in a red stole with the tassels in his mouth for flames.

"Don't dragons eat cream-cakes?" Julia asked.

The tassels dropped. "Well, yes. When there aren't any kings' younger sons around. Wiglaf! Tea."

The children took off the more hindering parts of their array and sat down, relatively quiet as they tucked in to the cakes.

"The reporters were maddening. Was I Dr Brodrick's fiancée? Why did I break it off? One of them suggested I was in love with Hussein."

"And are you?"

"No, of course not. Oh, I'm in a bit of a mess"—Julia wanted desperately to respond to the maternal effect this woman had on her, but remembered in time that Marion would be her professor's wife. "But it's nothing to do with Hussein, and it'll sort itself out anyway." She veered off. "I only hope that the University won't object to all this fuss."

"Why ever should they? It's only a journalistic lark."

"Well, Professor Kriss—do you know her?" Marion shook her head. "She's in charge of East African Linguistics. She was furious at Paul getting involved and her department being mentioned in the papers."

"It'll all be forgotten in two days. You didn't tell them anything, did you?"

"No." Julia laughed. "I never thought I'd have to use the term 'no comment' to journalists, but I did. Still, it isn't quite over for me."

"How do you mean?"

Julia gave the children some more cakes. In spite of their noisy games, they had been trained to silence at meals with grown-ups, and were unexpectedly well-behaved. "Oh, I don't know." Julia lit a cigarette and was silent. "I'm sorry, do you smoke?" Marion shook her head.

"Desmond Sykes asked me to do a paragraph on it for their Comment page. Anonymous, of course. Some line they had about employment of coloured people and mixed marriages. A symbol of the new natural liberalism in the younger generation. Hands across the sea and so on. In fact anyone could have done it, but the editor wanted a personal slant on Hussein, and Desmond couldn't ask Georgina."

"Dear old Desmond. How do you get on with him?"

"Oh, all right. I've been doing odd reviews for him."

"I know. I told him to use you."

Julia smiled, nodding her thanks.

"Did you write this thing?"

"Yes. It was for tomorrow's number, all in a rush. It wasn't until I'd put the telephone down after saying I'd do it that I realised—I suppose this sounds priggish and silly—that a few months ago I would have refused, without even having to think, simply on principle. I mean, one just doesn't use private knowledge of friends to make money—however paltry the sum may be—or even to help a newspaper grind its axe."

"I see."

The children were getting restless.

"Why don't you fold Julia's clothes nicely on the bed and then invent a new game? We'll be going home very soon."

"Can't we dress up some more?"

"I haven't got much else to give you," said Julia, "But you can make a tent with my counterpane if you like, and play at Red Indians."

"That's kid's stuff," replied Hrothgar with dignity. "I know. Let's play at The Wrath of Achilles. You be Hector." And with a most effective telescoping of *The Iliad*, he started dragging Wiglaf from the bed by the heels.

But Wiglaf roared his disapproval. "I don't like being Hector. I'm Merlin."

"Come on," Marion protested, "fold Julia's clothes and go and play by the table."

The children decided to take the clothes with them and withdrew.

"Look, my dear, aren't you making rather a lot out of a small incident?" Marion turned to Julia, pouring herself another cup. "May I?"

"Yes, of course, I'm so sorry. I expect you're right. It's just that—" she decided to let herself go after all, without actually confiding in detail —"well, it's all part of something bigger, a general lowering of standards. In itself it's nothing. But ever since I left the academic world I seem to have been assailed from all sides. All my values have been challenged and somehow haven't stood up to the challenge. It goes all the way through, in conversation, in scholarship, in beliefs. I didn't realise it till"—she paused—"the other day."

Marion looked at her thoughtfully. "But that's just part of living," she said slowly, "we all change our values, you know."

"No. You don't. Georgina doesn't. Paul doesn't. Don't get me wrong," she said hastily, "this has nothing to do with sin or corruption, or the state of my immortal soul. It's just a question of integrity in oneself, standing by one's own character and beliefs, whether they're right or wrong according to others. Even when I agreed to find Hussein and persuade him to leave I was acting against my own convictions. There are some things some people I admire simply wouldn't do."

Hrothgar came out, dressed as a warrior in her red stole, carrying a saucepan lid and the poker.

"Are you a Catholic?" Marion asked.

"I am!" shouted Hrothgar. "I'm going to massacre all the Protestants. I'm Saint Bartholomew."

"Oh, Hrothgar, do go away and don't interrupt."

Julia laughed. "I'm on Christmas card terms with God." Marion looked at her askance and she felt ashamed. "I came pretty near at one time," she said quietly. "And then—well, in a sense that's what I'm trying to say. Once you compromise with life over a big thing, you start compromising all the way along the line. And it cuts both ways. You find yourself giving in on little things, twisting words and meaning, always trying to be one-up on whoever you're with, and then suddenly you give in on something else, much bigger."

"But my dear child, that's life. Especially in the literary world."

"I know. But I'm beginning to feel I shouldn't take this job. I'm not temperamentally suited for an academic career. And I'm not sure that I want it."

"What absolute nonsense. The academic world isn't the cloister of sanctity you seem to think it is. It's as full of petty jealousies and shifting integrity as any other world. It's perhaps a bit more subtle about hiding them, that's all. Of course values change. I saw a play a while ago in which the word 'mummy' was pregnant with class hatred. Recently I read a novel in which the word 'mother' became more and more ominous and freudly monstrous. Sometimes it seems there's nothing left that means anything. But the reality behind the shifting values of words and feelings remains." Marion seldom made such a long speech and she poured herself another cup of tea.

"Mummy, what's a freudly monster?" The children had got tired of dressing up and were sitting around restlessly.

"One's self, dear," Marion replied, placidly.

"Oh, well, it's all in my stars," said Julia half seriously, opening the new issue of *Scopes and Horoscopes*. Marion looked at her with alarm. "*An underlying crisis in occupational issues.*" She laughed nervously. "They've got a new man this month, I don't like him."

"Some newfangled seer they've dug up?" Marion was smiling.

"I'm a seer," shouted Wiglaf and rushed to the table to get the green skirt.

"He says: *it would be advisable to avoid changes so far as possible and to keep all income-source activities on a good level.* Fat lot of use."

"Well, there you are."

Wiglaf emerged dressed as Merlin again. "You're going to be eaten by a dragon again," he announced, "and inside his tummy you'll find a prince, all made of fire and swords. But in the end you'll marry Uther Pendragon at the bottom of the sea."

"That's me," said Hrothgar.

"Well, you're not very cheerful."

"Merlin's never cheerful," Wiglaf replied gloomily.

"Look," said Marion, "I don't suppose I've understood the half of what you've been trying to say." Her tact was real, that is to say, unnoticed by Julia. Marion had in fact understood very well. "But it's clear you're going through a bad patch, whether it's emotion, intellect or religion, or all three. Let it ride, my dear, let it ride. And don't make any foolish decision now about a job you're not taking up till October."

It was six o'clock when they left. Julia cleared up the tea-things and then sat down with a cigarette, thinking that she had made a prize fool of herself. She thought of Paul with shame and then with anger at feeling shame. What right had he to be so sarcastically righteous, Bernard had asked afterwards. She had sent him away that evening and not seen him since. And now she wanted him, with an unrestrained, mortifying passion. Mortifying because she knew that it was Paul she loved.

She decided to go round to Georgina's. Hussein had found a room nearby, at Georgina's insistence in the face of the publicity and in the complex circumstances, but he would probably be there to supper. She marvelled at them both, and especially at Hussein. He had used the day of his disappearance with extraordinary efficiency, not only to go to the Zoo and buy a camel, first borrowing a large sum of money from his friend Sultan Ahmed, but also to get himself a job at the Technical School in the West End, teaching English to Sanuri and Isharood students. Sultan Ahmed, himself on a course at the School, was on account of his title much respected by the director, to whom he had introduced Hussein.

She met him at the corner of Warwick Street, on his way to Georgina's. He was wearing European clothes again and looked sad. "She tells me now she will not marry me," he said. "I cannot understand. She accepted Gedo and the silks."

Julia smiled and put her hand on his arm. "Let it ride, Hussein, let it ride."

"Gedo?"

"No, it's a proverb."

Hussein cheered up at once. "Explain it please."

"Well," she improvised, "when you're on a difficult horse which gallops away wildly or does unexpected things, you must hang on firmly and let it ride until it gets tired. Then it will be very gentle."

"That's a good proverb."

"Excuse me," a little man stopped them. "Are you Mr Abderlarky, by any chance?" He obviously came from the North.

"No, he isn't." Julia spoke brusquely and tried to pass. The little man stood in front of them, blocking their way on the narrow pavement. "I'm from the '*oodersfield Gazetteer*. I'd like to ask you a few questions, if you don't mind."

She suddenly recognised the door on her right. "Would you excuse us, we're going in here." She took Hussein by the arm and drew him in after her, hoping the man would have the sense not to follow them.

The little church had belonged once to the Portuguese Embassy and then to the Bavarian. It had been destroyed during the Gordon Riots and rebuilt, and was the only remaining Embassy chapel of the Penal times. Its square white walls and ceiling contrasted with the rounded alcove of the altar, which was of grey marble, domed with a colourful mosaic on a gold background. From the back of the church on either side, two elegant galleries strutted forward over eight white columns topped with gold leaved capitals. On the right, with an altar to herself, stood a tall statue of the Virgin, covered with a real veil, after the fashion of Mediterranean countries, and surrounded with votive offerings. An enormous candle-stand stood before her, flaring with many lights. The wooden pews on her side were never empty. Here in the silent little nave, the inhabitants of Soho would drop in, Spanish, Italian, French; fruit-vendors, bakers and coffee-grinders; prostitutes, hairdressers and restaurant owners. The workers of the West End would come and kneel or sit for a moment in their lunch hour or before trekking home, typists, salesgirls, businessmen and women: for this was Our Lady of Piccadilly.

Hussein was frightened. "I am not allowed," he whispered.

"Yes. She won't mind. Many people come here who don't believe in her. It's very peaceful. She dipped her hand into the font and crossed herself. They went and sat down. Julia knelt for a moment, her head in her hands, not praying. Hussein was gazing at the statue in some bewilderment.

"She is Our Lady," Julia whispered, sitting up again.

"Yes," said Hussein. "She is with us too. Mariam the mother of the prophet Jesus. She is in our pagan poems too, sometimes, they gave her name to Atete."

"Who is Atete?"

"She was a goddess. For fertility."

"I'm going to light a candle."

She got up and Hussein followed her. Very simply he imitated her gestures, put some money in the box and took two of the tallest candles. He lit them from hers, which she had lit from the others, and he placed them upright in the holders. "For me and Jojina," he whispered.

## Chapter Fifteen

THE heat wave was over. Camels, turbans, and exotic gifts were forgotten as the London sky once again piled its grey hair over the shapeless, comfortable tweed of streets, terraces, squares and crescents.

The press had not, after all, made much of the incident. The evening papers had splashed it excitedly in their gossip columns, where it competed, for a day, with an unknown starlet stepping on to a plane for nowhere interesting, or an average face gazing dully out of the newsprint as one of London's ten most beautiful typists. The dailies, having had more time to think, treated it as cold news, with commentaries on University life and its contribution to the breaking down of the colour-bar. Letters appeared for a while, protesting against the cruelty of keeping a baby camel in a Soho warehouse. One illustrated weekly ran a two-page feature, expanding the story and the photographs of Hussein, Georgina and the camel with a detailed account of Sanuri customs and a brief history of the country since the beginning of the British Protectorate. The newsreels cut it out, in favour of an international conference, Trooping the Colour, Ascot, and the heat wave on Brighton Beach.

Literary circles, however, took up the couple in a big way. Everyone wanted Hussein's exotic presence at their parties, and Georgina's poems, which had lain in editorial folders for varying lengths of time, suddenly appeared in five weeklies at once. Georgina, who had decided after all to consider herself engaged, come what might, was solicitously trying to protect Hussein from the onslaught of Western living, and to keep him to herself while she could. But Hussein was enchanted by all the invitations. Julia was also asked sometimes, and so was Paul. She always went, he always refused.

Desmond Sykes made the first important scoop by getting Hussein to read some of his poetry, in translation and in the original, at the July meeting of the Neo-Surrealist Group, of which he was the sombre secretary. It existed, somewhere in Bayswater, for the protection of free verse against the young rhymesters of the Neo-Augustan School. Middle-aged ladies, plain girls with earnest faces, and spectacled men in coloured shirts, looking like left-wing left-overs from the thirties, would gather once a month for rapturous readings of *The Waste Land*, *The Love Song of J. Alfred Prufrock*, *Hugh Selwyn Mauberley*, or loose translations from Appollinaire, Tristan Tzara, Aragon and, curiously enough, Ruben Dario. The black walls of the premises were covered with mediocre abstract paintings, jazzily contrasting with the "restless nights in one-night cheap hotels" and the typist's carbuncular young man, which could send such a pleasurable shock of recognition through that most liberal audience.

It was the last meeting of the season. Many more people than usual turned up, from rival factions and from no factions at all, to hear Hussein. Desmond was delighted, in his gloomy way, and put Hussein last in the programme. "Literary cliques," he said in his dirge-worthy voice, "were invented after the disappearance of bear-baiting." And with macabre glee he prepared to throw a party afterwards, and sent the assistant secretary out with a tall wine order. He quickly improvised a bar in the anteroom, on the table usually reserved for the hopeful exhibition of slim volumes, however, were still displayed on the bookshelves all round the room.

The packed audience listened, with varying degrees of interest, as Desmond's introduction of the evening's poets, who were sitting on either side of him, turned to a funeral oration in loving memory of free verse, free speech, free love and free intercourse between nations. Then a thin-lipped fat-faced man with grey hair wisping round his bald head got up and read a long poem abut the incestuous moon, who menstrually sphinxed her sterility:

"Pale prostitute of poets," he spluttered, "sleeping in secret with your brother Apollo."

A mousy girl with a tragic but monotonous voice produced a rhythmic account of a sexual murder, larded with detail and analysis of motive. Two women with cropped hair read a drearily idiomatic dialogue about fertility rites, between a drowned typist and Persephone in a suburban Hades, with squeaky contributions from a little man with a goat's beard who represented, on various levels, Pluto, the Fisher King, and a bank manager. Hussein listened intently, fascinated.

But he was the hero of the evening, and not only for his striking appearance. Nor was it just the way he chanted his poems on a repetitive tune, haunting but difficult to catch. Even through his loose and sometimes clumsy translations, which he carried entire in his head, something of his poetry's weird power and magic descended on his audience, growing a hush that opened like a flower in the soul of each listener, from the most urbane to the most blind.

The door at the back of the room moved ajar. No one turned and it shut again.

There was a tremendous ovation for Hussein. Wisely Desmond Sykes confined his vote of thanks to the words "thank you", which were charged with sepulchral emotion. They all adjourned, with much scraping of chairs and shuffling of feet, into the anteroom, where the murmur of dazed admiration was soon amplified into a roar. Almost everyone connected with poetry was there, from the grand-old-women-of-letters to the bouncy young men of know-how.

Hussein stood with Georgina and Julia, bowing to the congratulations and politely answering questions. Julia was in a trance. She had never seen so many well-known people at once. Names from the bookstalls, the review columns and publishers' advertisements suddenly acquired faces and voices which didn't seem to fit them at all. She felt both elated and unimportant.

"Oh, I'm writing a book commissioned by Tweedie and Tweedie," she told an editor who asked her what she did. "On mediaeval poetry." She tried to sound casual, but was glad of this small stage prop, which gave her some *raison d'être*, however hypothetical, in this literary assembly.

Then she saw Bernard struggling towards her. Surprised, then faintly annoyed, then pleased, she greeted him warmly. They had agreed never to take each other to individual invitations, and she wondered what he was doing here. He didn't particularly like Hussein.

"I tried to get hold of you before, but I came in mid-session."

"What's the matter, darling?" she spoke quietly in the uproar. He was looking worried.

"Nicolette decided to go to the college do after all. I called at your place to see if you were back. I felt lonely." He smiled at her ruefully and touched her hand. "I found this nailed on your door." Surreptitiously he produced a piece of black cardboard with a crude white drawing of a rectangle containing a skeleton and a leafy branch. Underneath were some strange signs in red.

Julia frowned. "I think these are Sanuri characters. I remember them from Paul's books." She shuddered. "I don't like it."

"Neither did I," said Bernard. "I hope it's not some sort of threat."

"But why me?"

"You should know."

"Oh, don't be silly. We'd better show this to Hussein."

They made their way to him. Julia whispered to Georgina first and they managed to get him away, not too noticeably, into a corner. He looked at the drawing and stood completely still. The whites of his eyes were enormous and even his dark skin seemed to grow pale.

"It is Ali," Hussein said at last. "He is here. He brings my father's curse."

Georgina held out her hand for the black omen, but he would not let her touch it.

"Why is it on my door, Hussein? What does it say?"

"It is a *tafriq*, to separate lovers, how do you say, in—in adultery." He almost choked as he said the word and shut his eyes, not noticing Julia's start. "There are two verses from Al Koran."

They were standing round him, protecting him from the jostling of the party. Georgina touched his arm. "Hussein, you must tell me what they say. This was obviously meant for me and I must know."

"I will not read it aloud."

"Please, Hussein," Julia insisted gently. "It has no power in translation."

He looked at her, startled into submission. In a low voice and with great effort, he read the words, translating as he went: "Evil on that day—to those who—treated—our signs as lies, who treated the day of judgement as a lie. This day will we forget you, as you forgot—the meeting with—this your day, and—your—er—dwelling—no, abode—shall be the fire, and no one shall be there to give you help." He turned it face down and said simply, "we must go."

Julia felt paralysed. Georgina still had her hand on his arm and after a silence which seemed like the still pivot of eternity in the centrifugal swing of the party, she spoke very calmly. "We can't all go together, it will be noticed. And we can't leave officially yet without questions being asked. Whatever happens, we must keep this quiet, you understand, Hussein? No newspapers."

"Yes, I understand."

"I will slip out first with Julia, as if we were going to the cloakroom. We'll get a taxi. You wait a few minutes, then go to your cloakroom, and come down as soon as you can. Don't get caught up by anyone, even on the stairs."

"Jojina, don't leave me alone." There was both terror and adoration in his gaze. She stood hypnotised.

"I'll stay with Hussein," said Bernard quietly, "and see that he gets out."

Georgina swung round in alarm.

"I'm sorry, this is Bernard Reeves. He found the—thing—on my door and brought it here." Julia lowered her voice. "You can trust him."

Georgina stared at them both, vaguely taking in the situation but too frightened to argue or distrust anyone. "Well, thank you. If you could yourself take the attention of anyone who waylays him, that would do it."

Ten minutes later all four of them were in a taxi, bound for Warwick Street. The journey was a silent one.

An exact replica of the drawing was nailed on Georgina's door. Hussein took it down, read it and placed it face down over the other one, which he held gingerly between his thumb and forefinger.

"Gedo is killed," he said without turning. The taxi drove off and they swung round to look at the warehouse opposite. Its door gaped at the precocious street lighting of the cool summer night. They ran across the street, Hussein following them slowly. Gedo lay dead on the bloodstained hay, with a spear in the hollow of his throat, just above the breastbone.

## Chapter Sixteen

THE rain was pin-pointing London's wet July on the windows of a double-decker bus. From the front seat on top, nothing could be seen but tearful dots that plucked the misty glass like exclamation marks, as the fuselage rumbled slowly forward over its invisible pilot. It was like flying blind.

Julia sat in silence with Bernard, feeling cold in her wet sandals. His plumpness pressed closely into hers as if to iron out the dampness of their coats with his weight. Because of the rain, he had abandoned his Lambretta in the Museum car park. They had left the Reading Room early and gone to the cinema. She hardly remembered the film and they had not needed the aphrodisiac picture-language of celluloid to teach them the romantic poses and gestures or the erotic approach of parted lips. Now he was taking her home to dinner with his wife. They would talk about his book, her book, and her mediaeval contribution to the symposium on adultery.

"Still like me?" He snuggled closer.

"Uh-hm." She gazed into the steamy window, seeing nothing. The bus was crawling down Shaftesbury Avenue in the much misnamed rush-hour.

"Oh, darling. I do adore you so."

"Do you, Bernard?"

"Our minds fit like hand and glove." The phrase seemed unpleasantly apt. "And our bodies—well—"

"Our bodies, yes."

"They don't do so badly, either." He gave a coarse laugh and pressed her thigh with his.

"I'm not very happy about it, Bernard."

A woman brushed his shoulder with parcels as she left the opposite seat to struggle down the aisle. "Sorry."

He grunted. "We'll manage, darling. Do you think I like snatched half-hours and necking in the cinema?" she shifted uncomfortably. So far she had enjoyed the necking more than the rest. "We both want more," he went on. "Oh, to take you away. To Spain. Days and days in the hot sun, all day together. And all night. Hours and hours."

She frowned. She noticed how much more positive he had become, how much less cautious. He never asked now if she loved him. In the beginning he had been charmingly uncertain, greeting her every day with his anxious "still like me?", which had become now a friendly formula. Then, as his passions had leapt beyond the bounds of fear, he would insist: "Do you love me? Tell me you love me, if only at this moment." And she would reply: "Yes, at this moment." But when he had begun to talk in terms of years, not months, of finding a key-flat, of meeting her in Spain next summer, she had smiled it off as day-dreaming. One day he had asked her, in all seriousness: "Would you marry me if I were free? I can't be, but would you? Is it that kind of love?" And she had answered frankly that it wasn't. But she knew he hadn't believed her, or had conveniently forgotten it. No-one could make love to him like that and not feel exactly as he felt. Imperceptibly, he had begun to take her love for granted.

"Hours and hours? You have Nicolette for that." The remark was in bad taste, but she felt annoyed. She tried to make it sound teasing by nudging his knee, but he took it seriously.

"Nicolette finished all that a long time ago. Oh, I'm not saying I was never in love with her, as many husbands do. I was, very much. But somehow she always managed to—well—you know. She's French, and never let me forget it."

Julia wondered whether married couples always blamed each other for their lack of skill or trouble in preventing the natural death of desire. She shrugged, unwilling to betray her secret sympathy for Nicolette. "If she were truly Latin, she would have brought out the best in you." She nearly added "as I did", but said instead, "it's there, after all."

"Yes," said Bernard smugly, "it's there." His hand crept under her arm and he fondled her breast, hunching up his shoulders to hide his gesture from the crowded passengers behind them. "Darling, don't worry. We'll find time and place."

"That's not what I meant. I just don't like the situation."

"Hmm. Clever of you, seeing we haven't got one. Comfortably non-situate, as the estate agents might say."

"You can skit over anything, can't you?"

His eyes flickered as he looked at her and she knew he was searching his mind for a joke. "Don't worry, I skit ever so phrenic."

She winced. "You know very well I was talking about Nicolette."

"Oh, darling, do stop dramatising."

Julia said nothing. Only his emotions and difficulties seemed to count. Hers were given easy labels, or otherwise dismissed with a crude joke or a pun. When he felt serious she had to respond, but when she felt serious he accused her of being solemn, he played with words, saying, if she protested, that humour should penetrate life at all levels and not form a separate compartment. Yet his own humour was mere flippancy, emphasising the very division within himself which he condemned in others. Bitterly she remember a sentence from her Aquarius "character": *Serious-minded, you dislike flippancy, and many will wrongly judge you to be without humour.* The true humour of life, Julia thought, should illuminate, not shut out, its essential melancholy, its macabre elements, and its fleeting moments of unbelievable elation.

"I'm uneasy about that African curse." She peered out of the window, rubbing a clear space. They had reached Hyde Park corner, which looked like a drizzly point-to-point of buses in hunting-pink, among a pack of panting small cars, frozen into immobility. "Why should it be on my door, and why should you, of all people, be the one to bring it to me?"

He looked at her. She was fingering her crucifix nervously. He had not noticed that she was wearing it again. "Oh, come. You don't believe in all that stuff?"

"I believe in almost anything."

"Evidently. And without evidence."

She turned on him. "You heard what Hussein said: to separate lovers in adultery. That applies far more to me than to Georgina."

"But it was meant for her. Which just shows how inaccurate this primitive ballyhoo can be."

She was silent. The bus droned towards Knightsbridge. "There's the same basic truth in all religions," she said at last, "both in the devilish and the divine. Christ recognised evil powers. And good magic, too. Hussein once told me that in the pagan Isharood tribes, the local wise man spits on the earth to bless it for fertility. There's a belief that spittle contains the essence of the man."

"An obvious sexual symbol."

"Christ put His spittle on the blind man's eyes."

"Are you turning dear old Frazer upside down to prove Christianity?"

"Yes. Why not? I'm glad you admit he's old-fashioned." Bernard grunted. "The same revelation exists everywhere, in different forms, from the start," she went on. "*The Lamb slain from the foundation of the world*, as St John says." She became aggressively emphatic. "All mediatory gods are lunar gods, with some symbol of horns, or lyres, or bows. Even Zeus killed a ram to disguise himself in its fleece before appearing to a human. And look at Plato's crucified soul of the world. Its point of intersection is the equinox, the constellation of the Ram." She paused and added dramatically, "Christ died in the constellation of the Ram."

"What have you been reading? Sounds like crank scholarship to me."

Julia shut her eyes and said nothing.

"Darling, I'm sorry." He edged even closer, twining his leg in hers. "I just don't see what all this has to do with us. We're in love, damn it. You're not taking anything away from Nicolette that she hasn't already lost."

The platitude rang ironically in her ears. Once before when she had objected to the deception he had charged her with being novelettish. "I wonder if you realise, Bernard, that the constant minimising of other people's small worries only makes them bigger? They get complicated by anger. And funnily enough, a little over-dramatisation, which only lasts a moment, makes them seem smaller, and fall into place."

"I know, my sweet, forgive me. You're tired and cold and wet, and everything seems horrid."

She tensed up again at his pressure and cursed herself for wanting him so much. No doubt everything had a physical explanation: it was the easiest. He was fondling her arm and she put her head on his shoulders.

"Careful, darling." He looked round at the busload of passengers and her hair feathered his chin. Satisfied by the anonymity of faces, he buried his lips near her ear and murmured, "I adore you, I absolutely adore you."

They sat in silence until the bus turned, more quickly at last, into the Fulham Road.

"Ah, Berr-narr. Hello, Juli-ah."

She hated her name when Nicolette pronounced it. The stress on the last syllable always sounded ironical and now the two "ahs" seemed to sandwich their names in subtle mockery. Yet Julia liked her. Nicolette, in her eyes, was a true scholar, like Jarvis-Anderson, like Paul. They had, it seemed to her, integrity in common. With all her angular aggressiveness, Nicolette was herself, a classicist maybe, but a complete person, and Bernard's wife. Julia's attitude to her had veered round several corners as her relationship to Bernard had changed. From a guiltless, easy admiration and polite friendliness, she had come to resent that harshly protective deflation of his personality. Then as they became more dependent on each other's tenderness, she had been thankful for Nicolette's inadequacies which made him turn to her. Now, knowing Bernard too well, she saw Nicolette in a different light, half blaming her for the cockiness he assumed when away from her, half sympathising with her treatment of him. Uncertain as to which was the result of which, she envied Nicolette her poise with him, her superiority and her intellectual independence.

"But you are wet. Come, I will light the electric fire. You must dry your feet, it is very dangerous to stay with wet feet." Her even stress of syllables made it all sound very dangerous indeed. "You will wear my slippers." She left the room and Julia sat down by the fire. Bernard gave her a whisky, touching her hand and smiling.

Julia's feet were rather lost in the slippers. She felt suddenly embarrassed, as if she had been caught *in flagranti*, wearing Nicolette's dressing gown.

"This terrible English climate," said Nicolette, "and no *chauffage central*. I am longing for our holiday."

"When are you going?" she hoped that her voice and eyes did not betray the sudden panic at the idea of not seeing Bernard for several weeks.

"To Italy." Nicolette had heard the more natural question "where?". Or had she noticed her alarm and misheard on purpose? Julia made an effort to pull her nerves together and took a gulp at her whisky.

"How wonderful. Whereabouts?"

"Ostia first. Then Herculaneum and Pompeii." She spoke as if modern Italy didn't exist and rhymed Pompeii with *mon pays*. "To look at the *graffiti*. I'm writing a book on them."

Bernard smiled wistfully and she remembered how he had grumbled about being dragged round Italy time after time. He had always wanted to go to Spain. Next year he would, on his own, he said. With her.

"Oh, I'd adore to see Pompeii." She felt a curious urge to side with Nicolette again. "I didn't know you were interested in archaeology."

"I'm an epigraphist." Her tone implied Julia had said something very naïve. But Nicolette always enjoyed *explication de texte*, especially when the text was her own conversation. "*Graffiti* means inscriptions on walls," she said kindly. "My book is not about Pompeii itself, it is an analysis of the social implications of those inscriptions."

"Rude ones, mostly," put in Bernard.

Nicolette did not shrug her shoulders, she *haussa les épaules*, her scorn seemed so very French. "There is still a great deal unexcavated. The *graffiti* give us evidence of elections, trade, scandal, gladiatorial shows, etceterá. They also help scholars to identify the streets and the buildings, the private houses, the temples—"

"And the *lupanar*." Bernard was evidently feeling reckless.

"That did not need identification by inscriptions," said Nicolette coldly. "Why is that the only thing people seem to know about Pompeii?"

Julia, in this respect, was "people". She swung to Bernard's side now, but wouldn't show it. "What about the men they found, preserved in lava?" she asked, to keep the peace. "Tell me about them."

"Oh, they're in the museum." She seemed to lose interest, but suddenly added, "they died in agony. One of them lies face down, hiding his eyes. Like us in the Blitz."

Julia's memory jolted unpleasantly. She put her hand quickly up to her own eyes, pressing them tight shut.

"Dar—don't you feel well?" Bernard nearly gave himself away.

"Oh, it's nothing." She paused and felt embarrassed. "That's how they found my mother, under a houseful of rubble."

"*Ma pauv' petite!*" Nicolette exclaimed and became very maternal. "Have some more to drink. You are tired and cold. Berr-narr, did you bring her on your horrible *motocyclette?*"

Julia remembered how useful the Lambretta had been for their afternoon escapades into the country, during the last warm days of June. She thought of the dismal bus ride and felt suddenly very lonely, homeless, a misfit in all societies. She was nothing to no man. Not even Penelope to Odysseus, she punned to herself now, bitterly imitating Bernard. She heard him protest and Nicolette saying, "what have you done to her?" Julia suddenly realised with a stab of self-hatred that her terror was not caused by the fact of that knowledge but by the tolerance and experience it implied. She saw herself, last on a list of lapses, and felt humiliated by her jealousy.

After dinner, they all washed up together. Bernard had been stoically witty during the meal, partly to cover his concern, partly in a sincere attempt to cheer her up. He brushed past her recklessly as they dried the dishes together, behind Nicolette's back, singing to emphasise his ease.

The rest of the evening was painful. Bernard rather fancied himself at German *Lieder*, and suggested a *musikalische Stunde*, with Nicolette at the piano and Julia as solitary audience. The songs he chose were crude with what he thought was subtle *double-entendre*. His untrained voice could switch uncomfortably from counter-tenor to a deep baritone, and he stood with his back to the piano, burning her up, he felt, with ardent messages in that most hideous tongue.

> *Ich lieb dich, mich reizt deine schöne Gestalt*
> *Und bist du nicht willig, so brauch ich Gewalt*

This was followed by a tremulous and tender *Bist du bei mir, geh' ich mit Freude*, a song meant for a soprano, on which his voice cracked drunkenly. The accompaniment was much more efficient.

Julia left early, pleading tiredness. "I do hope you have a splendid holiday. I don't suppose I'll see you before you leave." She addressed them both, keeping up the fiction. "I may go away to the country myself."

Bernard seemed alarmed.

"Good," said Nicolette, looking at her closely. "You need a rest."

"Well, thank you so much. You've cheered me up enormously."

"Let me see you home."

"I wouldn't dream of it. The 14 bus takes me straight to Bloomsbury. I'll be fine."

"I'll see you to the stop," he insisted, "it's pouring with rain."

"Well, it's very kind of you. Nicolette, thank you again."

"Are you really going away?" he asked as they stood at the bus stop. The rain was drumming its dark Morse on his umbrella.

"Yes," she lied. "I have some thinking to do."

## Chapter Seventeen

PAUL worked throughout the summer, ignoring the University vacation. He sat in his little room, correcting the proofs of his *Grammar of the Sanuri Language*. It was his fifth proof-reading and still there were misprints. Each time a line had to be re-set, a new mistake was likely to creep in. Paul felt sorry for the printers, but more sorry for himself. He had to invent special signs and modifications of the Latin alphabet to render the sounds exactly, the sudden aspirations, glottal stops and clicks which could change the entire meaning, even of a syllable. And the Department had insisted on a parallel transcription of all words and quotations in phonetic script, which hardly facilitated the printing problems.

There was a gentle knock and the door opened slowly. Paul and Hussein gazed at each other in silence. Hussein had known by instinct what Paul would think of his decision to stay in England and he had not come to see him since Paul's farewell party for him, two days before the camel incident.

"I am disturbing you?"

"Come in, Hussein. I'm very glad to see you. It's been a long time."

Hussein looked crestfallen. "When cows are about to go out, they lick one another. When men are about to die, they love one another."

Paul knew better than to minimise this as dramatisation. He accepted the love in silence and asked, simply, "which of us is about to die?"

Hussein sat down. He was fingering a large white envelope. "I will tell you a story. It is a funny story, but also very sad. In the world there are three misfortunes. The first is wealth, because it grows, and when it has grown, the king wishes to seize it for himself. Therefore wealth is a misfortune. The second is the woman. She falls in love with a warrior who kills you and flies with her to another country. Therefore the woman is a misfortune. The third is God, who has created us, one white, one red, and one black. Our father in the beginning was Adam, our mother was Eve.

We are all brothers. As God created us in the beginning, we should love one another, if we all looked alike. But He made us of three kinds, and we kill one another. Therefore God is a misfortune."

Paul smiled. He recognised the tortuous Sanuri way of coming to the point and let Hussein have his run in. He quoted a proverb at him. "God created the python; justly He also created the tree bark for medicine. He created love; justly He also created patience."

Hussein was not impressed. "It is very sad," he said, "that we have so many proverbs. One is against the other and a proverb can be found to prove anything we want."

"It's true they can be misapplied," said Paul, finding his cue. "For example, we are not killing each other now."

"You remember Ali, my brother-in-law?"

Paul nodded, relieved. Between two Sanuris the run-in process would have been much longer. Leading up to a request for a loan, for instance, might take two hours of colourful citations. He remembered Hussein interpreting for a magistrate who, after twenty minutes, had asked: "Well, what are they saying?" Hussein had replied: "Nothing, sir, they are just talking." He was more direct with Europeans.

"Ali came here three months ago. He took a job in the docks, but really he came from my father. He talked to me many times, telling me to go back. Because I had written to my father about Jojina."

"And you didn't listen to him?"

"Yes, I listened. For long hours I listened, hours as long as the road to the watering plain. But there was no water at the end, and I was thirsty."

Paul lit a cigarette and sat back. "What did Ali do?"

"He killed Gedo."

Paul recognised the name of an epic camel and connected it at once with the incident in Soho. "In the warehouse?"

Hussein nodded. "On the tenth day of Du-l-hiijjah. *Idu-l-kabir*, the Feast of Sacrifice. It is lawful to kill a camel by *nahr* with a spear in the breastbone.

"Even a wedding present?"

Hussein shrugged. "He killed, as you would say, two camels with one spear. That is sad, but not so sad. Gedo was not well in the warehouse.

He had not much air and I could take him out to walk only at four o'clock in the morning."

"How do you know it was Ali?"

Hussein put the white envelope on the table and gestured Paul to open it. Paul took out the black squares of cardboard and read the inscriptions.

"Where did you find these?"

Hussein told him.

"On Julia's door? Why Julia?" he frowned.

"My people are sometimes stupid," said Hussein sadly, "and sometimes clever. Ali read about me in the newspapers and he saw Julia's name, that she was looking for me on that day. He thought maybe I wanted two wives here. Or if one refused I would take the other. Perhaps he thought I did not want to go home and therefore I marry an English girl. But that is—you told me your proverb one day—to put the carriage before the horse."

"He must have written to your father." Paul read the double curse and shuddered.

"Yes. It is transmitted. Through the nearest male. I have no brother. Ali is nearest."

"What does this drawing mean? I thought you weren't allowed pictures?"

Hussein frowned. "It is *sih'r*."

Paul recognised the Arabic word for malevolent magic. Most of the magic in Islam derived from the Koran and used its very words, by which method it had acquired some degree of tolerant recognition.

"But how can your father—"

"This is a *tafriq*, which can sometimes be allowed, especially this one is even recommended. It is to separate lovers in adultery."

"I see." Paul thought of Julia. "Why the branch?"

"This is only a message, a report of what my father did. My father went to a green tree and wrote on a branch seven times *baduh* and cut the branch, saying he cuts the love of—a named person—from the heart of Hussein." He gave a little choking sob. "Then he buried the branch in the tomb of a dead man unknown and said the verses from Al Koran, and he added: let Hussein, son of Abdillahi, forget Jojina, daughter of England.

Let their hearts die like the man who lies in this tomb." He put his head in his hands.

"Hussein, if you obey your father now, can he undo this?"

There was a pause. "Perhaps. If I obey."

"If?"

"I love Jojina."

Paul sighed. Then he looked steadily at Hussein and said, "I love Julia."

The exemplary nature of this statement was not lost on Hussein. He shifted uncomfortably. "The Englishmen," he announced, proud of his generalisation, "their blood is more silent."

Paul wasn't going to argue on that one. Life was always supposed to be so much easier for those who controlled their passions. "On the other hand," he rejoined, "we don't have such terrible punishments. We have only our own will power to rely on. This should make the decision easier for you."

"A father's curse is a terribly thing," said Hussein slowly. "It may remain even if he undoes it."

Like some types of Catholics and, indeed, like Julia, Paul was deeply superstitious. He believed in faith as such and respected all forms of belief, from the prayer-wheel to the rosary, from the unlucky ladder to African voodoo, reserving his intolerance only for the Protestants. The Church is stingy with dogmas, he used to say to Julia, who could accept the zodiac but stumbled over the Immaculate Conception, we should be asked to believe much more. The whole point of faith is the impossibility of what's believed in.

And he had much approved of Hussein's naïve remark that the Pope should make it clear about Mary going bodily to heaven, surely it was a fact, not just an Assumption. Now he was shocked at Hussein's sudden lapse of faith in the power of words to undo as well as do. He told him the story of the prodigal son.

"I know," said Hussein, "but the prophet Jesus does not say what happened afterwards. The son perhaps was very unhappy at home. The father perhaps was reminding him always of his forgiveness, and the son was thinking again of the days in the big city."

Paul looked at him in dismay. Hussein loved stories and normally never queried their endings, accepting as given without ever misunderstanding their hidden meaning.

"Tell me, Hussein," he changed his tack, "what can be the effect of this curse on Georgina? The thing was on her door. Or Julia?" he added after a pause.

"A curse cannot touch the innocent," said Hussein. "Julia is all right."

Paul looked thoughtful. "And Georgina?"

"Jojina." He sighed. "I will protect her."

"So you admit that you are not innocent. That what you are doing is wrong?"

"It is wrong for my father. For me it is not wrong."

"But Hussein, if the curse affects you, because from your father's point of view you are not innocent, how will you be able to protect Georgina? And it will affect her too. You will both be unlucky and perhaps very unhappy."

"If I stay, the curse is on us. If I go home, the curse is on us. It is better to be together and fight it."

"How?"

"By not believing in the power of it."

This unexpected shift into Protestant subjectivity astounded Paul. The logic of it, too, was very shaky. On the one hand, the power of his father's curse was so strong that it could not be undone: it existed, like the Sacrament, whatever his thoughts or subsequent actions might be. On the other hand, it could be ignored or accepted, like a sacramental, according to belief: it could even be made null by mere disbelief. But he noticed that Hussein had stretched out his right hand as he spoke and remembered that the open hand was a talisman against the evil eye.

"In our Church," he said slowly, "the words for the undoing of a wrong are as powerful as the wrong was in the first place. Provided you believe it was wrong."

"It is not wrong," Hussein insisted.

"Perhaps not. Look at it this way. Your father's curse is the wrong. It is evil. You go home and show him that you forgive him, by loving him and doing what he asks. He repents and undoes the wrong. The wrong doesn't exist any more, because he's truly sorry. Surely that's easier than fighting it."

Hussein was not used to Jesuit sophistry and looked at Paul in amazement. The idea of forgiving his father was quite alien to him. "My father is not wrong," he said simply. "For himself he is not wrong. Therefore he cannot repent."

"Then you must be wrong," said Paul with implacable logic, "and you can repent. You once told me your Recording Angel rubbed it out if you repented."

Hussein crossed his arms over his chest and touched the angels on his shoulders. "Before eight hours," he said. "After eight hours, it is written."

"So you feel you might as well go on?"

"For me and Jojina, it is not wrong. Love cannot be wrong. It will be stronger than the curse of my father, who is also not wrong."

Paul sympathised with him more than he would admit, feeling his pain, physically, in every channel of his body, in the tightening of his throat, in the nervous centre at the back of his neck, in the burning of his eyes. "Have you thought of Georgina in all this?" he said at last. "What sort of life can you give her?"

Hussein flinched at the Englishness of this aspersion on his capacities. "I can give her love," he said angrily, "love she could never find anywhere except here." He thumped at his heart.

"That's just it," said Paul, looking at him squarely. He assumed a man-to-man tone. "You realise, don't you, that when a European girl has made love with a—Sanuri," he particularised to touch Hussein's national pride, "she can never find happiness with anyone else."

Hussein seized the table with both hands. "She will never love anyone else," he shouted, "she will never need to love anyone else."

"Not if you stay, of course." Paul kept his voice absolutely steady. "But one day you may find your religion is too strong. Then you will leave her and go back to your own country."

Hussein crumpled on the chair. "I will never go back. I have cursed my religion."

There was a long silence.

"I want to ask you something," said Paul at length. "For myself. When you said your father's curse had no power over the innocent, did you mean someone innocent of this particular business or innocent generally?"

"I do not understand."

Paul hesitated. He really believed in this curse and was upset enough to be indiscreet. "Whatever you may feel about the uniqueness of your love," he said slowly, "and about the weakness of our passions, Julia and I loved each other as strongly, as deeply, as you and Georgina love each other. Because of my religion, I couldn't marry her. Believe me, it wasn't easy, for either of us. But in some ways, it was more difficult for Julia. I had my religion, after all. But I could only control myself by not seeing her at all, and plunging myself in work. She had no work at the time. Her parents are dead. I know that she was very unhappy." He was fiddling with a box of matches. He took one out and struck it nervously, watching it burn itself out. "Now," he added with an effort, "she is no longer innocent."

Hussein was silent. "She was not concerned in my father's curse," he said after a moment. "It will not affect her. But she will never be happy except with you," he added, winning his point in the very parallelism that Paul had tried to apply to Georgina.

But Paul was relieved at his reply. "She may be. It's rather different. I have applied to be sent back to Sanuri in October."

This unexpectedly hit the mark more painfully than any theological discussion. The two years he had spent as Paul's assistant flooded Hussein's memory. He saw himself on the verandah of the small white villa where Paul had lived, teaching him the rudiments of his language, laughing delightedly at Paul's attempts to reproduce his pronunciation. He remembered their walks, the constant pointing at trees and shrubs, camels, horses, ponies, at a hornbill or a vulture in flight, at the pointed girdle round the hips of a woman who would turn shyly away. He saw himself introducing Paul to his family. "You will see my father." He looked troubled.

"Hussein, come back with me."

Hussein gazed at him with despair in his eyes, emphasised by the blue whiteness round the large black pupils.

"Look at this," said Paul, handing him his *Grammar*, which was opened at one of the translated texts at the back.

"*I cannot stay in this land,*" Hussein read aloud, "*where men have no white cloths over their shields, and no sword with which to greet a man. I will go to the Tshugal Valley, where the grass grows high and the men are men, who speak fearlessly with the Genii.*"

"Do you remember we translated this together?" said Paul softly. "It was very difficult."

"*I will hear the hoofs of my pony Djamar,*" Hussein went on, "*clattering over the ground like a grown girl who has been given a husband and great flocks. She has clothed herself in a costly robe, and in the midday shadows brings food to him, clattering in her shoes of cow's hide.*"

Paul switched on the recording machine. He had been checking the pronunciation of the poem that very morning. Hussein's voice wailed out of it, lilting and nasal, sobbing and descending and leaping up again.

"Jojina." Hussein put his head in his hands.

The door opened quietly and Angela Kriss stood watching the scene in silence. The record went on interminably, with all the refrains and repetitions that made Sanuri poetry so much longer in the original than in translation. Hussein's body was convulsed as he listened to his own voice. At last the song came to an end. The stillness was tangible.

Angela Kriss went up to Hussein and put her hand very gently on his shoulder. He didn't move. "You are among friends," she said softly and pressed his shoulder tenderly. "But you must go home."

He looked up. His dark face was wet and shining.

"Go home, Mr Abdillahi. Go back home."

## Chapter Eighteen

CATS were squalling along the garden walls behind Bernard's flat. Their screeches clawed at the night, striping its silence to a tiger skin, streaking across the jungle of twisted chimney tops to mate in the sultry air with other screams, hisses and wails from beyond the sleeping ocelot eyes of the stretched yellow houses.

The outsize continental furniture of Bernard's bedroom stood out, larger even than life, in the glimmer of August moon, like a clutter of Roman monuments at night in a very small *piazza*. There was hardly room to walk round the double bed: on one side stood a tallboy bearing shelves of books; on the other an old-fashioned wardrobe whose mirror scornfully threw back the chancrous light from the window onto the wall behind the bed; at the foot of the bed, the narrowest possible aisle was occupied by a low stool in front of dressing-table which took most of the window space. The curtains were undrawn, the window was wide and chequered, the ceiling low.

Bernard lay awake in the big bed. The time by the luminous clock on the side-table was half past two. He stretched out his hand and groped incredulously along Julia's naked body, sleeping peacefully beside him. She had turned away and lay on her side, her back arched, one breast falling over the other, her leg angled like the foreleg of a circus horse taking a bow. She woke, stretched and turned to him.

"Darling, darling," he murmured. "There's nothing quite like this. Naked, and all night. Waking up to each other."

She kissed him sleepily. Slowly he roused her again to the warmth of his body between the sheets.

"I adore you." Intense and low the sweet inanities of passion came tumbling out. "I've never, never wanted anyone so much, you do believe me, don't you?"

Julia never committed herself to drastic statements. She liked to make love in silence, talking with her hands, her teeth, her tongue, her thighs, with her crisp hair nestling in his neck. Only the quick panting and occasional moans, and the long, final animal wail gave hint that she had a voice at all.

They lay quiet at last, side by side, holding hands. For all Bernard's initial offer of his shoulder, which, she remembered, was there when she wanted it, Julia preferred to sleep unpropped. She had thrown out the pillow on her side.

"We both need hours and hours, don't we, my darling?" Bernard said to the moonlit ceiling. "We're hopeless with snatched half-hours."

Julia smiled in the half-light. How easily Bernard had shifted his early inadequacies to an excusable "we", a "we" distressed by the circumstances of time and place.

He lifted himself on his elbow and looked down at her face, intently aware of his debt to her but unable to express it. The moonlight thrown by the wardrobe mirror had moved from the wall to her side of the bed, whitening her skin and turning the bleached wisps in her hair blue.

"Darling heart. I do love you." She combed her fingers playfully through his hair. But this time he wanted more than silence. "Julia. Do you love me? Tell me you really love me, just once." He bent down over her, his lips butterfly-kissing hers, his hand wandering gently over her body. A new surge of desire made her raise her knees sharply. She abandoned herself to his caresses, though knowing he would not follow them up.

"Yes," she murmured. "I love you."

He kissed her gently and lay back. In a few moments he was asleep, breathing noisily but not snoring.

'This won't do at all,' Julia thought as the moonlight and her tingling senses kept her awake. What had started as a gay flirtation was turning into something much too complicated. She should have known that she was incapable of consistent cynicism, that she was bound, in her very nature, to become emotionally involved. She did not love him, no, but she was in love, physically in love, as she had never been before. And physical love, to her, meant its consequences: she wanted, in every vein and muscle of her body, to bear his children. At the same time, she disliked him more and more.

Julia had tried to avoid him. Since the poetry reading and that miserable dinner at Nicolette's the next day, everything seemed to have gone wrong. She had pretended to be away and worked in the Holborn Public Library. For two days: they hadn't got the books she wanted and the place was a solidified Ode to Dejection. She had stayed in her room, rewriting her thesis, and had asked Mrs Moffat to tell callers she was on holiday. But Monique Renaud, the French student next door, really was on holiday after her exams and had started to drop in, treating her as a Racinean *confidante* for the long and complicated plots of her love-life. Her hair was dark with a froth of dyed blonde curls on top, an exaggerated version of Julia's own carefully bleached wisps; and this annoyed her, as Monique's head looked like a glass of Guinness, which was not Good for her. The accent too, reminded her of Nicolette, and very soon Julia was driven back to the British Museum. And to Bernard. "Have you done your thinking?" he had murmured in her ear, bending over her desk with his face almost touching hers. "Oh, darling, it's been nearly a week." And the thinking had been undone, only too rapidly.

The shift in their relationship humiliated her. It was true that he had helped her at first. 'A man can spot a woman on the rebound,' she reflected bitterly, 'as a dog scents a bitch on heat.' But she had quickly gained the upper hand. If the jovial, knowledgeable examiner had soon been replaced by the gentle, avuncular protector, so had this father-figure given way as fast to the anxious lover, attentive with little gallantries, impatient every day to see her, transparent as to his motives and clumsy in his tactics. She had grown very fond of him. Then gradually, as she gave him back his sexual confidence, he had become—well, confident. She disliked the streak of coarseness which had been released in him, expressing itself in a relish for dubious jokes and frequent references to the peculiarities of past mistresses. He was more aggressive in discussion, hogging the conversation, interrupting, and easily debunking, everything she said with his wider learning. She had begun to feel small and stupid. She knew that the superficial good he had done her was being far out-weighed by the harm. She had shown him, and he had taken, only one side of herself. There was a whole area in her which he never saw, just as she wanted only a part of him. And when it peeped through the ramifications of their relationship, the branches quickly shut it out again. Concepts which still meant much to her, by which she had once lived, were swerved aside with a smart epigram, a pun, a quotation, a dirty story.

Julia, in fact, was fed up. Even on the level of a light-hearted affair he had become selfish, thoughtless in the little details and arrangements that make for smoothness in an unsatisfactory relationship. He expected her to be there when it was convenient for him, but would forget to let her know if it wasn't. At first she had thought it was mere incompetence. You can't run a love affair without attention the little things, she had said, they're just about all we have. In the worst circumstances one can *always* ring up. It's mere good manners. Are you so wife-ridden that you can't even go out for a drink, or a walk or to buy cigarettes? She was through with him, she had added calmly, meaning it. He had swung round in terror. "You're absolutely right." And he had made emphatic promises. Yet it had gone on and so had she. That he loved her, in his own clumsy way, she knew. But it was only in moments of intimacy that he was tender now. She had taught him to make love unselfishly and take his time. She had changed his rhythm and over-anxious, localised technique, and he had learnt quickly, gratefully. Nevertheless, he separated bed from breakfast with a complete and very English switch of personality.

Her head ached urgently, like a distantly beaten drum. Past conversations, every word he had said, even in unguarded moments, were relived in painful silence, conflicting with others, with her own mixed feelings, with the wretchedness of her desire, with the memory of different loves, different principles, and different conversations. How she envied men their vague memory for the details of their own declarations, of the words they had uttered in forgotten moods of humility, obsession, and adoration.

She tried to make her mind a blank. After using Hail Mary's, in vain and with some shame, as a sheep-counting device, she remembered a Yogi trick Paul had taught her: to imagine one is water, concentrating first on the fingers, trickling up the arms, streaming into the torso, flooding the legs, and gradually to become, everywhere, water. Julia, however, felt like a torrent. *Après le déluge*, she thought wearily, *moi*.

She woke with Bernard's voice singing in the bathroom. This morning it was a growling baritone, inappropriately enough.

*Ich grolle nicht*

*Und wenn das Herz auch bricht* . . .

She turned over, annoyed yet smiling at the memory of that absurd evening.

When she opened her eyes again he had switched to *Don Giovanni*. She got up and put her clothes on. *Cerca-a-te, cerca-a-te*, he wobbled, again in a tenor voice, as he went into the kitchen.

When she came out of the bathroom and joined him, the coffee and toast were ready. He pranced up to her and took her hand, singing *La ci darem la mano*.

*Vorrei e non vorrei*, she joined in as he led her round the table, *mi tremo un poco il cor*. They sat down gaily to breakfast.

"We've got all day in front of us," he said, "free as air. What would you like to do? I thought of going into the country," he went on without waiting for her reply, "But it's not all that sunny. There's the Klee exhibition I'd rather like to see, and we could try and get in to Brecht, either for the matinée or this evening."

"Oh, not Brecht."

"Not *echt* Brecht?" he quoted a drama critic's quip. Most of his jokes, she had learnt, were second-hand.

"I shall go to the Reading Room. I've got some work to do."

"Oh?"

"Yes. I can't go on wasting time like this."

He gave her a sharp look. "You're tired," he said gently. "Poor sweet. Have I worn you out?" But he looked pleased with himself.

"No. In fact, I'm going to work."

"But darling, this is our last chance of being together. Nicolette's coming back tomorrow."

"I know."

"Haven't you enjoyed these four days?"

"That's just it." She paused. "It was too easy."

"You mean you can't enjoy adultery unless it's complicated?"

There was a brief silence.

"Have you got a cigarette?"

"Here."

He took one himself and lit it, absent-mindedly, forgetting hers. She took the matches from him, pointedly.

"Darling, I'm so sorry."

"That's all right."

"Honey, what's wrong?"

She looked at him wearily. It was absurd, but tired as she was, she wanted him again. "I'm pulling out," she said simply.

He puffed furiously at his cigarette. "I suppose it had to come," he said at last. "But why? Why now?"

"I'm fed up."

"You mean you're tired of me? After the way you made love last night?"

She winced at this hackneyed blackmail on female sensual skill. "No. I'm not tired of you. Far from it. I suppose that partly I want to pull out before you're tired of me. But it's more than that. I'm fed up with the way you treat me—well, we've had that out before. And I don't like the situation. No, I'm not dramatising." He had been about to interrupt. "I'm being practical this time. We'll never have a chance like this again. Nicolette won't be doing vivas in Oxford every week. It'll mean going back to snatched half-hours and mucked-up arrangements. I can't take it."

"There'll be chances, darling. Unexpected ones. Be patient. Take a long-term view."

"I can't. I was already in a panic at the idea of your going on holiday in the middle of August. Oh, I know it started light-heartedly and you wanted to help me. But somehow it's all shifted." She paused. "It's not that I've fallen desperately in love with you, or want to break up your marriage, you know that."

"I know." He stubbed out his cigarette and gazed vacantly at the ashtray.

"It's just that now I seem to need you more than you need me. And I don't like it."

"It's not true, you know."

*The Languages of Love: Chapter Eighteen*

"Well, you make it seem so. Oh, not when we make love. But in little things. And little things are so much more important. At least, to a woman. I suppose you'll say that that's wanting it both ways. A woman revels in a man's respect and adoration while he's pursuing, and expects it to go on after she's become his mistress. It's the oldest story in the world."

"I say, you are being East-Lynnish."

She was furious. "You have easy labels to dismiss every shade of feeling, haven't you? But the feelings are just as real, however they're expressed. This ridiculous sub-Freudian idea that by naming a neurosis you'll cure it seems to have got in to everyone at all levels. You think that by giving an emotion a name that makes it sound silly, the emotion will go."

"No. But the effect of silly behaviour caused by that emotion is still one of silly behaviour. Otherwise you might as well claim that the feelings and convictions of madmen and neurotics are true."

"And so they are, to them. You can't treat them with smart labels. And madmen may be nearer to the truth than all you clever nitwits."

"Are you suggesting, dear, that you are going mad?"

"Not on your account."

"Well?"

"You humiliate me. Intellectually and in other ways. I seem to have no personality left. It's been invaded by yours, and I don't like yours all that much."

He tightened his lips. If in a way the accusations pleased him, testifying to his unsuspected power, they also made him angrily defensive, as accusations always do. "I'm sorry." He didn't sound it. He got up and cleared the breakfast things, taking them to the sink and washing them up noisily.

Julia was rather put out. She had expected at least some protestations of love or declarations of despair. "I suppose it was inevitable you should come to humiliate me, even unconsciously," she went on obsessionally, "because you found me in a humiliated position. You remember, when you offered yourself as a cushion"—she reminded him inopportunely of his ill-chosen phrase—"I told you that the only thing I couldn't take was the way Paul had cut himself off completely, just because we couldn't marry?"

"Yes." He clattered the cups on the draining board.

She got up and took a dishcloth to dry them. "Bernard, all I want is to stop being lovers. At least for a time. We'll have to anyway very soon, when you go to Italy, so we might as well now and it won't be so hard. But I want to go on seeing you."

He emptied the washbasin. "You just said I humiliated you, that you don't like my personality."

"I also said it had invaded me. It's like a drug, bad for me, but I must cut it down slowly."

"I'm not a thing, I'm a person. First you treated me as a medicine, now as a drug."

"You came to me as a medicine," she said bitterly. "You told me to use you. Though I was well aware it was only a way of barging in. You used me too."

"Use, need, want. What words. I was in love with you, damn it."

"*Was?*"

Bernard was silent. He walked to the table and lit a cigarette. Julia dried the last plate, very slowly.

"After all the things you've said, I don't see how you can expect a declaration of love. Or even want one. You don't love me, that's quite clear. You just want me, need me, use me, because I satisfy your lust." He smirked. "And all this talk of friendship. You've just refused even to spend the day with me."

She put the plate way and came to the table. "Only because I knew the day would lead to the night. I wanted a break. Oh, Bernard, don't you understand? I was going round the bend, I was falling in love with you, wanting too much. I got frightened." She stood very near him, her face in her hands. Why had it all gone wrong? Why was she declaring her love for him when last night he had been pleading to her, and she had decided that she disliked him so much?

He hesitated, then put his arms gently round her. "I do understand," he murmured. "Perhaps we shouldn't have had these four days. I was falling in love with you, too."

The past tense, though imperfective, was definite.

## Chapter Nineteen

"IT is with great pleasure, ladies and gentlemen, that I introduce to you this afternoon Dr Bernard Reeves, of London University." Paul spoke dryly, staring at the front row. He seemed to tower over Bernard, who was sitting down and wearing the smile of pleasure that should have been on Paul's face. "He is, as you know, going to read a paper entitled Problems of Linguistic Analysis in the Nominalism of William of Occam. Dr Reeves is a well-known mediaevalist and philologist. He has asked me, modestly I think, to make it clear to you that he is not by training or profession a philosopher, nor does he consider himself worthy of belonging to that more modern school of nominalists who call themselves Positivists."

Both men were soberly dressed in dark grey suits and white collars, but the contrast between them was striking. Paul stroked his beard gently as he spoke and had the air of an unconvinced saint interceding on behalf of a rather ordinary sinner at an indifferent heavenly assembly.

"Dr Reeves has long been interested in linguistic analysis," he went on, "and merely begs your charitable attention towards an amateur. As chairman I am forced to make this disclaimer on his behalf"—Paul's tone was more and more ironical—"because he has asked me to do so, but I feel sure that a syntactical analysis such as his title announces can only come from an expert, and that what he calls amateurish in his approach will prove to be a stimulating liveliness which is often absent from more expert work. Dr Reeves." Paul sat down abruptly as desultory clapping broke out. Bernard got up, bowed to him, put on a nominally serious expression to match his subject, and started.

Julia looked at them both with some dismay. The meeting was ill-attended, and although she had slipped in late and taken a back seat, she was easily visible to both of them in the small Council Room chosen for the lecture. It had never occurred to her that Paul would be in the chair. She had come, obsessionally, to catch a glimpse of Bernard, perhaps to talk to him afterwards. Indeed, she hadn't even known till that afternoon that Bernard would be speaking. Angela Kriss had met her in the Reading Room.

"You look dreadful, m'dear. Anything wrong? Why don't you come to the Congress? It'll cheer you up no end."

"What Congress?"

"British Philologists and Linguists. It's been going on for two weeks, weren't you in on it?"

"Well, I'm hardly qualified to attend."

"Nonsense. It's all dwindled to small sub-committees and seminars. Most of the non-Londoners have got tired of it and escaped to do some sight-seeing. There's a paper on William of Occam this afternoon, which should interest you as a mediaevalist. Dr Bernard Reeves, d'you know 'im?" The professor didn't notice Julia's slight start. "Friend of mine. About time a philologist tackled the philosophers—they've reduced all philosophy to linguistic analysis without knowing anything about language."

Julia smiled. She didn't quite see how Bernard's type of historical phonetics was going to throw light on conceptualism.

"I thought philosophy had become the handmaid of science, as it was once the handmaid of theology."

"Don't you believe it, m'dear. It's now the favourite courtesan of General Linguistics. Much more fun."

She remembered now that Paul had been asked to help organise the Congress, and to read a paper himself on new methods in African Studies. How long ago it seemed when he was sharing his plans and interests with her. But why should he be introducing a philosophical paper? Was he replacing someone else or was he, as a Catholic, interested in the Nominalist heresy? He certainly couldn't have chosen to put himself in such an awkward position. Yet, she reflected, perhaps he didn't know that the man in her room had been Bernard. He had only met him once, at Angela's party, long before anything had happened. But intellectual circles were a sounding-board of gossip, and besides, Paul was no fool. No: there was no doubt about the bitter sarcasm in the tone of his introduction—or was she translating everything she saw and heard into the language of her own emotion?

Language. The word sprang at her too often from Bernard's rich and varied voice. He was a good speaker. How strange, thought Julia, that they should have communicated so little to each other. They had talked of mediaeval poetry, of sound-changes, of methods in textual criticism; they had talked about problems in the books they were writing, and even about the subjects of the books; they had talked about people, about love, about themselves. Yet here was a whole area of Bernard's mind which he had never revealed, just as she never spoke of her interest in theology and comparative religion. Surely the age-old problem of the relation between intellectual concepts and things existing outside the intellect was also, like her own problem, one of belief in signs? Could they not have communicated through the language of belief, belief in the meaning of the words they used?

She tried to listen more attentively. Was he attacking Nominalism or defending it? He had opened his lecture with a clear exposé of the problem in classical and mediaeval philosophy: Plato's exaggerated Realism—reality outside and above the sensible world; Aristotle's Moderate Realism—reality dwelling in the midst of the sensible world and universal concepts faithfully representing the realities which are not universal; the third answer in the Conceptualism of the Stoics, sensation being the principle of all knowledge and thought only a collective sensation; the development of the Aristotelian doctrine by the early Scholastics, the decisive stage marked by Abelard and John of Salisbury; the early beginnings of Nominalism from Porphyry to Roscalin of Compiègne, finding its extreme form in the Conceptualism of William of Occam. The abstract and universal concept was only a sign, a label which had no real value since the abstract and universal did not exist in nature.

Bernard was a good populariser and obviously an experienced lecturer, adapting his material to the regular academic fifty minutes, with a beginning, a middle, and an end. Julia had an uncomfortable feeling that his paper was rather bogus, that he himself would be contributing little. Without any knowledge of the subject she could recognise the symptoms of potted scholarship and facile divisions. From seven years of University she had learnt one thing: that one learns little or nothing from lectures, even by the most eminent men. What had to be simplified for oral delivery was more honestly presented visually, and the sources used by the lecturer were more rewarding than what he made of them. Moreover, since the papers read at Congresses were always published later in the Proceedings of whatever Academy was holding the Congress, the sole advantage of such organisations seemed to be social. And if emotional complications prevented the lecturer from meeting a particular, very particular though unimportant part of his audience, why have a Congress at all?

Now he was analysing the Latin of Porphyry's famous question: *sive subsistent, sive in nudis intellectibus posita sint*? The Nominalists had concluded that universals were *nuda intellecta*, purely intellectual representations. Julia looked at Bernard, feeling naked, wanting his naked body and his naked intellect. Why, oh why could the sexual act fail so lamentably in giving possession of another's mind? He had invaded her, yes, but only by destroying, and the part of her which had collaborated with him was left condemned, alone and without a master. She glanced at Paul, who sat very still, staring intently at the carafe of water in front of Bernard. There had been no shifting meanings behind the labels of words. The word was the thing.

"The role of the universal is to serve as a label," Bernard was quoting William of Occam, "to hold the place in the mind—*supponere* is the word he uses—of the multitude of things to which it can be attributed. Now what precisely does *supponere* here mean?"

She couldn't catch his eye. Had he noticed her? What does a lecturer see in an audience, especially in such a sparse audience? Faces like scattered leaves in an autumnal tree? Eyes flitting like buzzing dragonflies on a drowsy summer day? Bloodless shades feeding on his words? Paul was paler than any shade and would not look up. Bernard's blue eyes swerved over the anonymous faces, leaving his paper, returning to it, and swerving again at each new paragraph.

Question time became the usual farce. No one kept to the subject of the lecture, and each query was an excuse for a verbal dissertation on the questioner's pet ramifications. Julia experienced a wild and heart-thumping urge to ask something marvellously clever, just to make them notice

## The Languages of Love: Chapter Nineteen

her. But she had no philosophical or linguistic hobby-horse to ride.

A large man in a light blue suit got up. He wore rimless glasses and a spotted bow-tie. He even coughed with an American accent.

"Janleman. S'rr. I believe it was Minahvski who said that the ethnagrapher's perspective is the only one pahssible for the formation of funnamennl linguistic conceptions, where-ass the philahlogist's poin'v view is fictitious and irralevant. Would you agree, janlemen, that we now have to adahpt a nahn-Aristotelian arritood to language?"

A chair scraped as someone tried to interrupt, but the nasal twang calmly went on, about mathematics as the only non-variable language, about the structural differential, Euclid, non-Euclid, non-Newton, and a non-elementalistic language. Julia looked at Bernard, who was listening carefully, as if to a foreign language. He had always attracted her most when he concentrated. She wanted to merge with the subject of his attention, and when his attention had focused on her, she responded like an open book. Now he had put her away on a shelf, she was a language he had brushed up and wearied of, bored by its facility or by his own proficiency.

"W'rrds like true, folse, prahperty, to know, to hate, to lerv," the American went on, "and an endless procession of the most imporrant terms we use, must be considered as multiordin'l and, janlemen, ambiguous." Julia saw Paul and Bernard exchange glances and smile awkwardly. "Their meanings are depennent on different but unspecified orrers ahv abstraction. It is no exaggeration to say, s'rr, that most tragedies, private, social and racial are innimately connected with the nahn-realisation ahv the multiordinality ahv the most imporrant terms we use. Janlemen, S'rr. I thank you."

Bernard looked a little nonplussed and a woman started giggling. Angela Kriss rose to insist that modern linguistic methods worked in full cooperation with ethnography and anthropology. The discussion was moving further and further away from William of Occam. Then a gaunt young man who had been trying to catch Paul's eye managed to extract a querying "yes" from him. Julia wondered where she had seen him before. Some students' gathering, probably, or the Mediaeval Society. His voice cruised on one low uvular note.

"Scepticism is always ultimately a scepticism of the word." He cleared his throat with a more promising velar sound, but went on in the same gear of monotonous nasal precision. "Any period of empiricism is inevitably accompanied by some form of Nominalism." Paul suddenly relaxed and was smiling at last. Julia listened intently, though her eyes were fixed hypnotically, not on the speaker but on the two men at the lecture table. How close would the young man get to her own failing trust in the meaning of the words each of them had used?

"The inseparability of the word and the thing," the young man whined on, "is the first premiss of all positive forms of culture, while the loosing of the word from the thing is the beginning of scepticism and relativism, Sophistic scepticism had already left its mark on Plato. I cannot think," he added dryly, "why the modern version of disbelief in the word calls itself positivism, when its main assertion is that the word is not the thing."

The American half rose from his chair but sat down again, quelled by a nasalisation of pitch that rivalled his own with a truly British conviction of superiority. I love them both, thought Julia, I hate them both, two different loves and hates all going by the one name of love. What had the American said about mathematics? Non-Aristotelian, non-Euclidean, non-elementalistic. Meaningless negative notions sprinted across the bracken of her brain, crackling their unreal concepts. Love was a theorem proposed by silence, love was the corollary of absence.

"In the beginning was the Word and the Word was with God." Julia started. The young man still spoke as if he were checking a ledger aloud with a chartered accountant, but this was the largest amount so far debited. "Trust in the word is not only the key to mediaeval culture, it is the bridge by which a way to the nature of the Deity is found. Nominalism thus becomes, for this culture, the most fundamental of all heresies." He suddenly seized the back of the empty chair in front of him and spoke with even greater precision, so quickly and forcefully that he now quacked like an excited duck. "The low evaluation of language in Hegelian philosophy produces mere labels, behind which meanings can be quietly shifted. The whole mystery of the word is that it is multiple, in many languages, just as the Sacrament is multiple, and yet uniquely identifiable with the thing." Julia saw Bernard smile and suddenly hated him.

Of course the man sounded ridiculous, but—"Depart from this," the voice quacked on, "and you get semantic anarchy, chaos, war."

He sat down at last. Only about six people were left in the room and Paul brought the meeting to a close. Bernard had coped very deftly with the questions by implying, correctly enough, that they were not questions at all but interesting contributions for which he was truly grateful. His smile was disarming and his lecturer's manner smooth. During the clapping, which sounded like five frogmen flapping on a rock, Julia urged herself, unconvincingly, to slip away, but sat transfixed by her own desire to make him look at her. He was drinking water and talking to Paul.

"Like to meet the lecturer?" Angela Kriss brusquely snapped the beam of her attempted telepathy. Julia flinched.

"Well, actually, I have met him. At your party last spring. Besides, he was my examiner." She couldn't face the irony of being introduced and preferred to risk not speaking to him at all. "I have to go, I'm afraid," she added, suddenly terrified at the prospect of confronting Paul and Bernard together.

"Oh, my dear, I'd forgotten," Angela exclaimed. "How tactless of me." For a moment Julia thought she meant Bernard, and stared at her in dismay, followed by shame and a nostalgic longing for Paul and her engagement days. She shook her head, inside which despair struck small and cold and sudden. No communication seemed possible with anyone. She waved uncertainly at the professor and walked towards the door.

Outside in the corridor she bumped into the gaunt young man. He was putting on a macintosh, although it wasn't raining.

"Ah," he said venerably, "I was hoping to find an opportunity of having a few words with you. I trust you will excuse the liberty. We did once have a very brief conversation—a passage of arms one might say—in an espresso bar, *The Groves of Academe*, if I remember correctly."

She looked at him, searching her memory. "Saint Thomas Aquinas!" Suddenly she remembered.

"Well, hardly." He introduced himself and sounded more like a duck than ever.

She smiled faintly. "I'm sorry if I was rude."

"Not at all; not at all. I should not have interrupted. But you were talking rather loudly, you know, now and again." He suddenly looked very kindly at her. "I am sorry you are so unhappy." The nasal tone had soothed itself down almost into a purr.

She was embarrassed. "I was interested in what you said just now, about the meaning of words changing behind the labels." She stood there uncertainly, wondering if he was going to invite her to a theological coffee session, and he obviously couldn't make up his mind just what he wanted to say to her.

"Yes." He took up the cue gratefully. "That's how it all started. The word became a mere sign. Then, instead of the Bread being the Body, it became a symbol, with purely subjective significance. Symbolism replaced metaphor, nominalism replaced realism. Ha! Nothing is any more!" He gripped her arm and peer at her intently. "Who do they think they are?"

Julia gazed at him in alarm, half fearing the glimpse of fanaticism in his piercing eyes, half welcoming his absolute faith. "But it's true," she stammered, "it is all relative. We can't communicate."

"Ha!" he exclaimed again. "Is that a pun? You are right. There is no communion, with God or man, because we have lost faith in the word. We have all gone mad. Do you know what the Spanish is for mad? *Incommunicado.*"

She felt suddenly isolated, an untranslatable meaning hiding behind a label. At this moment the door of the lecture room opened and Paul came out with Bernard, walking straight into her. "I'm sorry."

"Hello." She stared at him wildly and then at Bernard. Inside the room Angela Kriss was arguing with the American. Bernard looked much more annoyed than Paul, yet even this hurt Julia less than Paul's gaze of crushing, intolerable compassion. "I enjoyed your paper, Bernard. Congratulations."

"Thank you."

She hesitated, then introduced the theology student, hoping for a smoother conversation, about symbols, sacraments, words, labels, language, anything rather than this complete collapse of communication. But he had recognised Paul and decided to take himself off, mistaking his cowardice for tact, and with a clerical assumption that having sown the seed of truth in Julia's soul he could leave the harvest to nature.

"I didn't know you were interested in—er—theology?" she appealed to Bernard in a desperate attempt to bring his mind close to hers once more.

"I'm not. Your friend seemed to be, though."

She was silent.

"How are you?" Paul asked, unable to disguise the conventional query with his gentleness.

"All right, thank you. How did you come to be in the chair?" Her curiosity overcame her caution. "This isn't your usual line."

"I know." His answer matched the ineptitude of her last remark. He seemed to make an effort and added, "I was asked to."

"Paul—" she started and then changed her mind. "Did you enjoy it?"

"Yes. And no." Bernard was looking restless. "We must go, I'm afraid," said Paul. The "we" was like a small dagger in her throat. "There's a party—"

"Yes, of course. I—I'm sorry to have kept you."

"Goodbye, Julia."

"'Bye. Goodbye, Bernard."

"Goodbye."

They walked away together. She knew now for certain that they had both seen her come in, had both, for different reasons, been irritated, had both studiously avoided catching her eye, and had both been relieved to see her leave the room. The two men she loved, who had loved her, were now, through their very dislike of one another, in league against her, silently, far beyond the spoken word. The bitterest humiliation to a woman was the basic, unconscious, primaeval comradeship of men.

## Chapter Twenty

*POUR se distraire de son malheur en philosophie, Mathilde voulut être parfaitement séduisante.*
In spite of her scholarly training in objectivity, Julia was feminine enough to see herself, or aspects of herself, or what she thought were aspects of herself, in every novel she read. She was sunbathing, and put her head down on the open copy of Stendhal, feeling, at the moment, more *rouge* than *noire*, though the last two weeks had been *noires* enough. She thought of her life as a student, neatly fitting in her doctorate as a *malheur*. Julia was by no means self-confident about her achievements, whatever Professor Jarvis-Anderson may have said. She felt she had bluffed her way for long enough, and now her other self was calling the bluff.

She was trying to catch up on reading all the books everyone seemed so conversantly familiar with. Out of pride or inferiority, she had insisted on specialising much too early, eager to use her government paid university training for something she couldn't possibly do on her own. Now she felt she knew nothing after 1400, except what she had read in her teens. And that was ten years ago, when the war seemed so much more exciting than books. Methodical by nature, she was now "doing" French 19th century novels, one author at a time. She played with the sentence in her mind, thinking of the last few weeks, and turned it the other way about: *Pour se distraire de son malheur en séduisance, Mathilde voulut être parfaitement philosophique.* No, it didn't sound right.

She sat up, streaming with sweat, and looked at the packed sausages of human flesh lying around her, in various stages of cuisine, from the raw to the darkly grilled—most of them, alas, raw, the English summer having been what it usually is. Plump and shapely in her red swimsuit, Julia herself was medium done, for she had acquired a first coat in the June heatwave, which had come so conveniently just as she had finished her specimen chapter for Justin Jacob. Now the late August sun had unexpectedly scattered the leaden clouds, revealing a forgotten blue sky above, pale but clear, like that of a late Mediterranean afternoon. And Londoners, together with Julia, flocked gratefully to the Lido on the Serpentine.

It was astonishing how many people seemed to be out of work on that day. Spivs had deserted their barrows, housewives their sinks, thin clerks had closed their ledgers and shopgirls had left their counters unattended. It was as if all the districts of London had synchronised their early-closing day.

Julia had come, oddly enough, with Desmond Sykes. After the poetry-reading he had tried to find out from her, in vain, why she had left so suddenly with Georgina and the guest of honour. It had been, he said, most humiliating for him. Since then, he had become ghoulishly attentive, and today had taken time off from *The Platform* for the frustrating pleasure of lying near her, half-naked, on the worn out yellow grass of the Cockney Riviera. He did not look like a ghoul, however. The pink of his face changed abruptly to white at the neck, and with his apple-green trunks he reminded her of a Neapolitan ice. He was certainly melting almost as much. He had removed his half-spectacles—she had expected him to wear semi-sunglasses—and sat there, blinking at the bright light out of minutely wrinkled sockets.

"All these beautiful bodies," he moaned, looking distractedly, now at the boys, now at the girls. His eyes might well have squinted apart with bisexual interests. "I am old. And you, my dear, are young, vital, warm." He put his hand on her back, which was certainly warm. His fingers wandered to her neck.

"Desmond, dear. I'm very fond of you, but do stop pawing me."

"So bedworthy and so puritan." He sighed a deep stage sigh. A gramophone, a pocket wireless, and the shrieks of young people who were tossing an enormous rubber ball at each other, made conversation difficult. Julia lay back, facing the sun, thinking tragic irony.

"I assure you I'm neither," she said, and closed her eyes. A rich coloratura was crooning from the gramophone.

> *Don't know why*
> *There's no sun up in the sky*

> *Stormy weather*
> *When my man and I ain't together...*

She lay absolutely still, passively giving herself to Bernard. She had never been passive with him, but now in her imagination he made love to her, all over, and she didn't move. She cursed herself as every kind of fool. She had broken it off, long before she was ready, at the wrong moment, just when he had learnt to relax, just when they had found something which was out of this world, just when they loved each other most. She should have let it ride, she thought, let it ride, it would have tamed itself. Was she then capable of loving fully only *in absentia*?

She decided to go in for a swim. Desmond followed her, entering the fluoride water like a cat, frightened of getting wet. She dived in and swam far out, glad to be alone in its cold, rushing embrace. The worst was over, she thought as she floated on her back. She no longer went to the British Museum expecting to see him, she no longer waited in the evenings, hoping he would call, by telephone, or in person, penitent and pleading. The telephone. She had come to hate it as a nerve-wracking and satanic instrument, which had for a time carried a voice that turned her inside out, and which later was silent, or rang, electrocuting her veins, only to bring other voices, usually for other lodgers. Now he had gone away on his holiday, she felt only a quiet agony, a constant presence which was not too unbearable.

A satanic instrument. She swam back, thinking of the black omen from Africa, remembering Paul; remembering almost with wonder their childish happiness and her swift, easy and fully convinced enthusiasm for the Church; and that first rehearsal for her present pain when he had cut himself off. If this is a repetitive process, she thought cynically as she walked, shivering slightly in the breeze, to the small patch already occupied by Desmond, I should get used to it. Next time I'll know how to cope. But she felt ashamed.

*So THIS is the Garden of Eden*, the pocket wireless was blaring to the conflicting tune of *Bewitched, bothered and bewildered* from the gramophone:

> *Behold on the threshold we stand.*
> *Pass though the portal now,*
> *We'll be immortal now,*

*Hold—my—hand.*

The theology of popular songs seemed as mixed up as her own.

"You've been gone a long time," Desmond growled, and added in a submarine voice, "very Freudian, the love of water."

"You must be an Adlerian, then." She flung herself down.

"So cold, water," he said gloomily, "so wet."

"Desmond," she asked when the sun had warmed her again, "there isn't by any chance a minor editorial job going on your paper?"

"My dear girl, if there were, I would suddenly become very, very popular. Which would be extremely pleasant. Just think of it. All those young would-be poets eating out of my hand." He savoured the daydream for a moment. "Alas!" he added tragically, "it wouldn't even be up to me in the end. Honourable Mrs Robin Trout is a literary snob. She wants names."

Julia wondered what Desmond had done to get a name, if he had one. Perhaps he had acquired it by writing very clever books in the twenties, and then lost it, somewhere in the reviewers' jungle, which produced its rapidly growing cubs so much faster than the old tigers died. "But surely such jobs can't be all that coveted?" She was genuinely astonished.

"In literary life, my dear, everything is coveted by someone or other." The pronouncement had a Doomsday ring about it. "But why do you ask? You're about to start a brilliant academic career."

"I'm not sure that I want it."

*Wanted*, echoed the gramophone,

> *Someone who kissed me,*
> *And said she loved me,*
> *Then went away ...*

"But my dear enchanting creature, many of us would give our eyes for a comfortable sinecure like that. Some of our best lit critters are only as good as they are because they can say what they like protected by a regular income and hiding way behind red brick."

> *... She was last seen*
> *Hiding out in someone's arms ...*

"You know nothing," said Julia, "if you think that these jobs are sinecures."

*He knew nothing*

> *Of the danger of her charms ...*

"Why does everyone always find an ignoble explanation for merit?" she went on. "If they're as clever as you say, couldn't it just be because they're clever? They're probably good at their academic jobs too." Desmond was one of the few people who brought out her own honesty and simplicity without expecting a mask of apologetic smartness.

"You're right, of course, my dear. I was speaking as a failure." He started elegising. "I'm an old man, and I've seen them come and go, boosted and dropped. Not that I can grumble, I was boosted myself once. Foolish people, critics, always so sincere in admitting they were wrong to praise."

"But surely it's never the same lot who boost and drop a man?"

"No, no. The juries change. Unfortunately."

A jury, the song's refrain was taken up for the second time, to give the fans their money's worth:

> *Would find her guilty*
> *But I'd forgive her*
> *If I could see-ee*
> *A signed confession*
> *That she was sorry*
> *And really wanted no-one but mee-ee.*

Julia smiled grimly. "Sounds like a mock-trial, doesn't it?"

"With mock-tribulations, though."

"This is what's happened to the fine legal metaphors of Provençal poetry," she observed sadly. The song had made her think of Paul, then of Bernard, then of Paul again.

"That would be a good subject for a book: *The Decline of Imagery*. Why don't you write it?"

She smiled. "I might, one day."

"You gorgeous bundle of brains and beauty." His hand wandered again, almost out of habit. She removed it gently. "Look, my dear, if you're really serious about literary journalism, you should meet more people. That's how it's done. It's slow but the only way. One mustn't push, one must just *be* everywhere."

"That's more easily said than done."

"Why not start now? I'm giving a little *soirée* at my flat in Chelsea.

Only a few friends, mind you. I'm very selective. I think the English will all go to hell, if there is a hell, for having invented the cocktail party. Or was it the Americans? Same thing, anyway. Hell will be one continuous cocktail party with nowhere to sit down and no-one filling the glasses, and everyone dragged off to meet a bore as soon as he makes any headway with anyone." Desmond was swept away by his lugubrious fancy. "And the host, who must not be named, will go round with a viscometer, measuring the success of his party by its stickiness."

Julia laughed. "Who will be there?"

"All the sour milk of London society—publishers, editors, authors, agents, script-writers, film producers, businessmen, débutantes—"

"No, I mean, at your *soirée*."

"Oh. Well, the Honourable Mrs Robin Trout for one. And the editor of *Metamorphosis*. I want her to come round to something like his policy. She won't, of course."

"What's she like?"

"She knows simply everyone. She takes people up for a time with sudden, inexplicable, and usually wrong-headed enthusiasm. If she likes you, she might help you a lot."

Julia let the gaffe pass. "You said there was no room on *The Platform*."

"Oh, she never lets her temporary enthusiasms affect her policy on *The Platform*. But there are other platforms."


The Honourable Mrs Robin Trout in fact hardly spoke to Julia. She arrived late, unexpectedly petite and ash-blonde, with a twisted mouth and hard blue eyes which could transform her faded ugliness to beauty when she laughed. She must have been at least forty-five, but looked ageless, and hugged a half-dozen long-playing records in garish covers, protectively, like a schoolgirl.

"I've got some new ones." Her voice tinkled excitedly. "I had to trail them round to a dinner-date. So sorry I'm late. We must play them. All of them. They're *bliss*."

Jazz had become very fashionable among the intelligentsia. Not modern jazz: England had just discovered Louis Armstrong, who had reached and passed his prime in the thirties. Solemn little Satchmo parties would be given in regency drawing-rooms. Critics, scholars, and poets would jig, poker-faced, to his subtly distorting rhythms and the triumphal *vibrato* of that agonised trumpet. And they would stop, of one accord, when the vocal came in, like a steam-roller on pebbles. "Listen. You can't dance to this. Isn't it heaven?"

Julia tried to jive with a radio actor who was playing narrator now, too, and shuffled helplessly after her with a wet lankiness masquerading as fawnish charm. He talked, smoothly, of verse drama, of Brecht, and, when he learnt that she was a mediaevalist, of François Villon, whom he knew well from a recent programme of translations in which he had taken part. Julia said shamelessly that as far as she was concerned, Villon was much too modern, the beginning of decadence. She freed herself as soon as she could.

Desmond, on the other hand, turned out to be a surprisingly good dancer. He had a fine sense of rhythm, and without actually jitter-bugging, steered her round expertly.

"Enjoying yourself?"

"Mmmm."

"I'm sorry it's not an intellectual *soirée* after all." He had to boom in her ear to rival the drums.

"Just as well."

"Oh, you wonderful body." He tightened his grasp.

"Isn't this *bliss*?" piped The Honourable Mrs Robin Trout over her shoulder as she jog-trotted past with the editor of *Metamorphosis*, who looked like Glaucus and danced like a fish.

"Relax your grip, Desmond. This is jazz, not a sex-mooch."

"Dancing, my dear," he announced sepulchrally, "was invented for the delicious frustrations of the contiguity of limbs."

"How like a man."

He breathed on her neck. "And contiguity with your limbs, my dear, is almost too frustrating to be delicious."

*Why, why, why?* The veiled sonority of Lester Young's tenor saxophone wailed as Desmond pressed against her. She felt too tightly uncomfortable to argue and merely repeated, pointlessly, "how like a man."

"If you go on comparing me to a man I shall begin to believe I am one." He released her a little and started swaying his hips to the hypnotic rhythm of the full swing style. By an unconscious X-ray through his clothes she remembered the Neapolitan ice and laughed.

"If the language of the learned is becoming more and more sophisticated," she said, "our vernacular is pathetically mock-primitive as a means of communication."

She left, by an unfortunate mistiming, together with the actor, who called her "my dear" all the way down the street and "darling" all along the Embankment, talking of Lorca's play, *Blood Wedding*.

## Chapter Twenty-One

"This is my bus stop," Julia lied to get rid of him. "Thank you, and goodnight."

"Darling, wherever can you live? I didn't know any buses went along the Embankment."

"The 39. It goes to Bloomsbury." It did, too, but a long way around.

"I want to take you to the theatre. How about next Wednesday? I can get free tickets."

"Well, it's very kind of you, but—I'm going away tomorrow. On holiday." One lie seemed to lead easily to another.

"You break my heart. Where? How long for?"

"Istanbul. For two months." Lies, moreover, became more improbably as one was added to the other. He gazed blankly at her for a moment, then put on a subtle look, which was rather lost in the sparse street lighting of Chelsea.

"Darling, I don't believe this is your bus stop."

"You win." She laughed. "But I can get home this way. And I'm too tired to walk to the King's Road now."

"You look very beautiful."

She grimaced. "Are all actors so fast and forward?"

"I'm not being forward, darling. That's just a statement of fact."

"Well, thank you again for seeing me to the stop. Please don't bother to wait."

"But I shall. Moreover I'll see you home. For one thing, I must know where I can get hold of you."

"You can't. I'm going away."

"To Istanbul."

"Yes."

"Do you know that I absolutely and utterly adore you?"

She swung round in alarm. By an actor's instinct, he had exactly imitated Bernard's voice. Or had Bernard's voice been imitating the stereotyped intensity of a stage love? She found herself wondering whether this young man was as skinny as his well-cut clothes and dandy waistcoat were so obviously trying to disguise. From recent associations she imagined him in bathing trunks. It was not an overwhelming concept. "You don't even know my name."

"Julia Grampion. I asked my author and host."

She didn't press for his.

"Mine's Marcus Valentine."

It fitted. The name sounded vaguely familiar from the *Radio Times*. "Well, it's been nice meeting you."

"Darling, there are hundreds of things I want to talk about with you. Religion, for instance. Are you religious? Everybody's religious these days. Fascinating. I just know I'll end up in the church."

"The church?"

"Roman, of course. The only one worth bothering about if one's going to bother at all. Don't you think so?"

Would that bus never come? She looked past him towards Battersea Bridge. To her amazement a familiar figure was standing at the parapet, looking down at the river, unmistakable outlined in the orange gleam from the illuminated edge of the Pleasure Gardens and the red light of the Hovis clock. "Hussein," she shouted, "Hussein."

He swerved round. She waved and shouted again. He crossed the road towards her.

"Julia." He came forward and shook her hand. "I am very pleased. I went to the British Museum today, to find you and say goodbye, but you were not there."

The actor narrowed his eyes, registering first the British Museum as a place where she could be found, secondly the friend, and lastly the fact that he was saying goodbye.

"You're going home?" Julia asked.

"Tomorrow."

"I'll come and see you off then."

"The ship he leaves very early. I have to go to the dock of London at six. Perhaps you will walk with me now. It is very sad."

Marcus Valentine was looking rather put out.

"I'm so sorry. This is Mr Hussein Abdillahi. Mr—er—Marcus Valentine." Hussein bowed, the actor nodded. "I'll have to leave you now, Mr Valentine." She spoke quickly, not caring what he thought, grateful to Hussein for delivering her and upset by the news that he was leaving after all. "My friend is going to Africa tomorrow. Goodbye."

"Au revoir, darling. Have a nice time in Istanbul." He waved lightly, pleased with his exit line, and walked off in long, self-assured strides.

They turned towards the Albert Bridge. It was after midnight and the fairy lights that laced its webbed suspension had been switched off. Its four towers stood dark and tall in metallic robes, Matthew, Mark, Luke, and John, each at one corner of the sleeping bridge and the dreamy river that passed beneath it. Four guardian angels, with wings of steely silence.

"I'm very sorry you're going, Hussein."

"I am sorry, too. I came to say goodbye to your river. She is beautiful and sad, your river."

Julia had not seen Hussein or Georgina since the omen incident. She had tried several times to call on Georgina or ring her up, but without success, and she had thought it best to leave them to their problems.

"Will you ever come back?"

"I do not think so. In many years, perhaps, when I am very old. What the wind has blown away is not found again."

"It wasn't just the wind, Hussein."

"No. It was the thunder, much thunder, which now is in my heart, roaring like a black-maned lion."

Julia was silent.

"Look. The new moon. It is a new month for us. Safar. An unlucky month."

"Why unlucky?"

"When the wounded camels are healed and the last of the pilgrims have vanished, and when Safar has passed, then the Umra is allowed for those who undertake it."

"What is Umra?"

"The little pilgrimage. We should not travel in Safar."

They sat on a bench overlooking the river. Upstream, the night was

## The Languages of Love: Chapter Twenty-One

feeling its way blindly along the whispering Braille of urban blocks. Tall chimneys pointed upward like a black hand in sinister blessing, and the roofscape twisted its fingers in a desperate deaf-and-dumb code to the silent sky.

"And Georgina? How is she taking it?"

"Jojina. She went away. Very soon. To her family by your lakes in the North. She likes lakes, they are like Japanese pictures, she says. She writes poems like Japanese poems, very short, about the lake. So short they are like our proverbs. They were printed here." He took out a page of *The Platform* from his wallet. "Paul showed me. The lake and the pine-tree. But it is too dark to see." For once he didn't recite poetry by heart.

"Hussein, has it been difficult for you without her?" She knew what a woman went through, and wanted to hear that a man could suffer too.

"I have waited for my boat five weeks. And every day of those five weeks has been a knife slowly twisting in a wound. It is not better now."

There was no stiff upper lip nonsense about Hussein. Pain was pain and love was love. He did not protest hyperbolically that he was swooning, sickening, dying, as a fair knight was bound by convention to do in days gone by. But neither was he euphemistic: he didn't care for, become fond of, want, need, like, it wasn't merely physical or just intellectual or platonic or romantic; he wasn't having woman trouble or getting her out of his system or sorting himself out. He simply loved and suffered, like everyone else.

"Paul has been very kind. He lent me some money for the ship, because I lost the money with the other ship. I will pay him back in Sanuri."

"In—Sanuri?"

"He is coming to Sanuri in October. For another year, working."

She was silent.

"He was worried about you," Hussein said gently. "He asked me if my father's curse could make bad luck for you. Or make you bad," he added, looking at her curiously.

"What did you say?"

"I said no, because you were innocent."

"Innocent?"

"He asked so too. I mean innocent in my quarrel with my father."

"But it has made me bad, Hussein. Or rather, I was bad anyway, after I couldn't marry Paul. But I didn't even mean that sort of innocence, I meant the corruption of the heart: love mingled with hatred, with constant humiliation. The desire to be superior on both sides, to be smarter than the other. You don't have that, Hussein. Proud as you are, you meet others in tenderness and humility." She looked sadly at the river. "Smartness poisons the heart. In that sense, your father's curse brought me bad luck."

"With that man?" He made a movement of his head towards the bus stop where they had met, and looked profoundly disturbed.

"No. I only met him this evening. He's a fool, and I was trying to get rid of him."

"Julia. The white women, they always turn to someone else, afterwards?"

She flushed in the dark. "Georgina won't," she said after a pause.

"But she was not innocent in my father's curse."

"She is a true innocent," said Julia. "I'm merely naive. And vain, and selfish. Georgina's different."

"You are stronger than you think, Julia." He turned towards her and said very gently, "pray to your guardian angel."

There was a long silence. The night was warm, as warm as when Hussein had called out the very same words to Justin Jacob, as if the tropical heat itself were wafting the message out of deepest Africa, a message from primitive man to the civilised white people of the West.

"Jojina is back," he said at last. "I saw her light. She thinks I have gone, but there was delay with the ship." He had his arms crossed over his chest, his fingers touching each shoulder. "I walked and walked. Like the night when I said goodbye the first time and stayed."

"You mustn't go to her," said Julia softly. It was easy to say. Bernard was on his holiday. There was no temptation to try and seek him out. But there had been, and she knew there would be again, and she didn't even love him as Hussein loved Georgina.

"No. I must not. Julia, help me. I have to face the whole night."

The proposition didn't strike Julia as odd. She had known Hussein a long time. "We will walk together," she said. "It's nearly one o'clock.

That's only five hours. I'll come to the docks with you. Are your things packed?"

"Yes. All on the ship now, except one small bag, in my room."

"You still live near—I mean in Soho?"

"Yes."

"Well, we'll have breakfast at the all-night restaurant in the Piccadilly Corner House. Then we'll collect your bag and take a taxi to the docks. We'll need it by then, I'll pay for it, and give you breakfast, too. Your last night in England: you must be entertained as a guest."

"Julia. You are a friend. You are a very good person."

They walked and talked, for three hours in the almost moonless summer night, down the river to the floodlit buildings, the Tate Gallery, Lambeth Palace, Westminster, across St. James' Park, the Mall and up into Piccadilly. They sat on many benches, moving off at the sound of heavy steps. They sat below the sprightly threat of Eros as the bright alphabets above and around leered their inane messages in glorious Technicolor to an empty circus. A policeman approached. They walked slowly up Shaftesbury Avenue and as far as the British Museum, which stood massive and mummified by the sultry black air. It was a quarter to five when they got back to Soho.

An early morning mist hung low over the Thames as the taxi drove across London Bridge. Some thirty cranes mounted guard on the South Bank from Hay's Wharf to the Tower Bridge, and several small tankers nosed each other along the quay, playing at porpoises and whitings to the large white snail of a ship further up. The taxi turned left down the flanking of dirty brick buildings called Tooley Street, and left again into the cobbled lane, lined with warehouses, which led in to Mark Brown's Wharf. Julia paid the fare while Hussein, who was carrying one small zip-bag, looked sadly through the dark passage that framed a square of sky, distant towers, white prow and water.

Inside the big black shed dock workers and stevedores were shouting and clumping around the row of small offices partitioned off with glass. Paul was standing at the barrier.

"You didn't tell me Paul was coming," said Julia as the two men waved at each other.

"No, I did not." He smiled. "I wanted my two best friends in England to say goodbye together."

She was troubled by the ambiguity of the sentence, but said nothing. Paul was visibly surprised to see her with Hussein.

"Hello, Paul. You see, I got up early too." She wasn't going to allow any ambiguity to creep into the situation. He looked at her brown but tired face, distrustfully, and then at Hussein, whose quiet dark eyes reassured him. And Paul felt ashamed of his thoughts.

"How kind. I'm very glad to see you, Julia."

Hussein smiled at them both. "Perhaps your guardian angels will meet again and fold their wings together. Perhaps one angel is less severe than two."

Julia looked away towards the river. The Tower of London gleamed its ancient white permanence from the opposite bank, beyond the gently rocking prow.

"Is that your ship?"

"Yes. He is Japanese. He is cheaper than the Birrtish."

The red sun on the Japanese flag flapped limply in the faint river breeze, doing fatigue for the one missing from the sky. Below it, a set of black ideograms made the ship's side look like one of Ezra Pound's later *Cantos*. Julia was reminded of the solitary poem on Georgina's wall. "The letters look so sad, going downwards."

"It is like po-ettery," said Hussein. "To fly up you must first go down."

"You sylin', mite?" said a docker, apparently to Julia. She smiled.

"No. Our friend here is leaving."

"Time's up, mite."

They walked onto the quay. The cranes were angling in the sky, some of them creaking with surprise at having fished such weird bundles and packing-cases from the troubled morning clouds.

"Hussein," said Paul. "I hate long farewells. When you go on board, we won't wait to wave. You understand?"

"Yes. A wave is very far, like a bird who cannot be caught. But it is the dove of peace.

"The seagulls will accompany you at sea for a while," said Julia. "They will be our farewell waves."

"Tell Jojina, please, I send her a dove of peace, from the sea."

They shook hands. Paul suddenly put his arms round Hussein and kissed him on both cheeks, continental fashion, much to the astonishment of the dockers. Hussein bent down and touched Julia's brow with his lips, holding both her shoulders in his hands. "Pray to your guardian angel, Julia. Goodbye. And prosper."

When he had disappeared beyond the gang-plank and into the ship, Paul and Julia walked slowly through the shed, back to the narrow alley of warehouses.

"I hear you're going to Sanuri, too."

"Yes. Next month."

"Good luck, Paul." She gazed at the cobbles as they moved under their feet. "And I'm sorry. About—everything."

"I know."

He took her arm gently and they stopped for a moment. "I'm very unhappy, Paul." He pressed her arm, but said nothing. "I don't know how it is, but I seem to have betrayed everything I ever believed in." She looked up at him, then beyond him at the name of the lane in which they stood: Potters Fields. " 'Ere, you can't stand 'ere, mite. The vans 'ave to get by."

A narrower lane, called Pickle Herring Street, ran parallel to the river, back towards Hay's Wharf, its buildings linked by brick transoms labelled with loading-heights, one prosaic bridge of sighs after another, each marked with the burden permitted. They walked along in silence.

"In spite of—everything, I still love you." Her voice was low and she seemed to be counting their steps, hypnotised by each foot as it came forward.

"I love you, too."

A dock-worker whistled at her. The clanging and banging became suddenly deafening. They passed a notice with an arrow which said H.M. Customs, and another warning them to Beware of the Cranes. At last they were out in Tooley Street, making their way to London Bridge Tube Station.

"You going by the Underground?"

"Yes," he said.

"My best way is by the 17 bus." Fatigue swept up her legs like quicksand as they waited at her stop. "Paul. Couldn't we still—I mean, you said there were two ways in which people—compromised. I wouldn't mind. Either way. Now."

His eyes were troubled. "We're both overwrought, Julia. I'm leaving next month. A year is a long time."

"Yes."

"The summer's been bad enough. Like a nightmare."

"Or an allegorical dream-vision?"

He looked at her very tenderly and put both his hands on her shoulders, as Hussein done. Like him, he kissed her gently on the brow. "Yes," he said. "An allegorical dream-vision. With Hussein as the moral meaning."

## Chapter Twenty-Two

"*MA DONNA!*" Marcus Valentine obviously didn't know much Italian. Julia had told him she was married, which was partly true and which had produced this appellation. But it hadn't put him off at all.

"So am I," he said. "My wife's on tour at the moment. She plays the cello, didn't I tell you? Doing very well, bless her heart."

Julia looked bored.

"But tell me about yourself. I suppose your husband's in Istanbul."

She couldn't help smiling, and nodded.

"Darling, I absolutely adore you."

She wished he wouldn't imitate Bernard's voice so well, and looked across the foyer at the small groups of people in conventionally unceremonious clothes—two women in slacks, girls in cotton dresses, men in lounge suits, light jackets and neck-scarves. Only one couple was in evening dress.

"Wonderfully effective, so far," said a voice behind her, "don't you think?"

"I don't know, old boy. I wasn't moved, you know, not moved."

"How about you, John, were you moved?"

The third bell rang and they went back into the stalls. His free tickets were for the first row, rather to the side, and being so near destroyed the theatrical illusion for her. She could see every stroke of greasepaint on the actors' faces, the line on the brow where a wig ended, the tattiness of their mediaeval costumes, the dust raised from the floor as their feet pattered across the stage. The set consisted of one surrealistic Gothic arch and a tall ladder, and she could see into the wings, which looked much the same. But Marcus Valentine enjoyed the closeness. He hardly listened to the play and whispered professional comments in her ear, on this actor's voice production, that one's double-take, another's uncertainty of exit. It was a verse-play in an experimental theatre, a Master

Builder theme supposedly transferred to the Middle Ages by means of a mock-Elizabethan English, the illusion of which was further destroyed by words of more recent origin like *mesmerised* and words of current fashion like *ambivalence.*

Since the jazz party, Marcus Valentine had given her no respite. He had found out her address from Desmond, who must have relished the *Schadenfreude* of his new role as Pandarus. The working hours of radio actors seemed conveniently erratic, though no doubt, she thought cynically, this one could also, if it suited him, suddenly become tremendously busy. She remembered the pain when she had rung up Bernard at his college, after the break and before that appalling lecture: his diary was completely full up at the moment, he had said with a fake apologetic tone. He had found time enough when he wanted it. Now Marcus Valentine was turning up on her doorstep, waiting for her outside the British Museum, and her loneliness was overcoming her natural repugnance.

*And now you turn all my creative plans*, the frustrated architect ranted, *Into perpetual pangs of poetry without The pleasure of conception or the joy of birth.* A gross caricature of an inquisitorial prior walked carefully downstage, rubbing his hands. *Your art must serve only your love of God. You are but clay in comprehending Hands, And absolute obedience to His laws Fashions His love out of your selflessness.*

Julia shut her eyes and closed her mind to this sanctimonious parody of the mediaeval spirit. Marcus Valentine was certainly trying hard to adapt his haphazard culture to her tastes. Men always did, at first, but in the end it was always the woman who took up the subject, or the slant on a subject, or the language of the man she loved. She remembered a girl who had studied Serbo-Croat, then Sanskrit, then Egyptology, according to the man of the moment, each man getting older as the subject receded in time. But men merely put on the superficial plumes of common interests. Valentine's trained memory was easily retentive and he had even quoted some Provençal at her, out of a recent and much mispronounced Third Programme venture. She winced at the reminiscence. They had eaten a pre-theatre sandwich in an espresso-bar off Great Compton Street. A skiffle group—consisting of two guitarists, a thimble-fingered drummer with a wooden washboard, and a man sweeping a carpet-brush rhythmically over three metal strings drawn taut across a saucepan—was producing curious calypsos in a darkened room decorated to look like hell. Luminous green eyes, flaming red tongues and golden horns peered from black recesses. The place was so packed it was impossible to get served, and those lucky ones who had cornered a table and managed to get a cup of coffee were unable to drink it for the numerous and tightly trousered bottoms that swayed past or, more often, plonked themselves down between the cups. The strumming was lost in smoke, chatter, and frequent screams of laughter. Troubadour poetry seemed rather out of place, even when whispered in her ear:

> *Sols sui qui sai lo sobrafan quern sortz*
> *Al cor d'amor sofren per sobramar ...*

"Oh, do stop this," she said, "you're too absurd."

"Darling, that's unkind. No one is too absurd to fall in love. Love is absurd. Didn't you know?"

"As a matter of fact, I did."

"Well then, darling." He put his lanky arm round her, awkwardly turned her face towards him and deposited a cold wet kiss on her lips.

She moved away. "It so happens, however, that the absurdity of love in general does not apply to us in particular."

"Why? You said I was absurd." The logic was too pat to be worth refuting. "I like being absurd," he went on, "in love. Love is a force, a torrent no thought can stop, a pining unto death."

"What romantic nonsense. Dregs of the Catharist heresy."

He looked rather put out. She enjoyed applying Bernard's technique to him.

"I adore you," he repeated, for want of a better answer. And again Bernard's tone echoed in his voice.

At last the play was over. She felt tired, depressed, and very hungry. He hailed a taxi and directed it to a small Spanish restaurant, which reminded her of Bernard again. "I'm all for keeping to the Romance Languages, even with food," he said in the taxi, and took her hand. "Especially since you're a mediaevalist, and have filled my life with romance." She took her hand away.

"Look, I'm sorry if I've misled you." She turned on him, sitting up straight. "I admit I'm lonely and unhappy at the moment, and I let you take me out. But please stop behaving as if we were madly in love. We're not."

"But I am. Oh, darling."

The taxi lurched and she fell sideways towards him. He grasped her and missed her mouth as they jolted forward again.

"I adore you," he said lamely.

"Well I don't adore you."

"You will. It's the man who must do the hunting." He put on a hungry look, and said intensely, "I'll make you love me."

She looked at him in astonishment. In spite of her twenty-eight years, Julia still tended to believe what people said. She stared at his dark chestnut curls and his pasty complexion, lurid in the dim Soho lights that glimmered through into the taxi, and for a moment she thought she might even come to this. This was what the Church's ban on her marrying Paul meant. She would go from man to man, each one worse than the former, each one comforting her inadequately for the previous loss. She had even flirted with Desmond, though he didn't count—any flesh would do for him. But in her present mood she thought herself capable of anything. Even Marcus Valentine. She felt suddenly furious. Then the taxi stopped and they got out.

"I mean it," he said when he had paid the cab-man. He took her arm and they walked into the restaurant. The smell of oil cooking thrust into her nostrils and she felt almost faint with hunger. It was very hot inside and she sat down at the table with relief, not caring where the conversation might turn.

"You'll have a job," she said in a flippant tone. "For one thing, I'm happily married, and a Catholic." She heard herself sheltering mendaciously behind the Church with surprised horror. Had the years under Paul's protection put her so out of practice? Could she not deal efficiently with an idiot without resorting to lies?

"But that's just what fascinates me!" he exclaimed. "It makes it all so much more complex." She gave it up. "Weren't you entranced by the play?" he went on smoothly, "the conflict of love and duty, selflessness and self-assertion. Love is wonderfully strengthened by conflict." He put on a very solemn expression and took her hand across the table. "Don't you believe that love conquers all? If one has loved someone deeply, one always loves her. Even if one never saw her again, the love would continue to exist, in the abstract."

"What utter nonsense. If you really believe that," Julia added, removing her hand from his, "here is an ideal opportunity to prove it to yourself. From now on you won't see me again."

"I'll die if I don't see you again."

"Die, then."

He was relieved at what he took to be a quip. "*Ma donna*," he exclaimed dramatically, "so cruel and so *lontana*."

Julia got up, suddenly nauseated, by him, by herself, by the verbiage that covered nothing. Her hunger left her. She felt she couldn't stay with him one moment longer. "It's *donna mia*, if you must speak Italian, and I'm staying *lontana* from now on. Goodbye." She pushed the table aside to get out.

"You can't leave now. We've ordered dinner."

She had a great desire to slap his face with an even wetter fish, but decided her bad manners would do instead. Julia ran all the way to Charing Cross Road and leapt on a 14 bus just as the lights changed to green. It was ten to eleven. The cool September night glowed pink above the neon colours, but she felt hot and angry and ashamed. Advertisements for the safest brands of contraceptives flashed in red lights from small shops. *Look your best in clothes*, said a large notice in an American menswear store, and she wondered what American men normally wore. A very tall policeman was gazing curiously at small satin ballet shoes in a window. The world seemed very incongruous, and Julia wanted to cry. Bernard was back and she had to see him. It was a quarter past eleven when she rang the bell at the flat in Drayton Gardens. Nicolette opened the door.

"Juli-ah."

"Hello, Nicolette." Her heart was pounding and her brow felt icy. "I—I've just been to a party round here and—I thought I'd call—on my way home—to see how you were. I saw your light." She was aware of giving too much explanation and went on lamely, "I hope I'm not disturbing you?"

"No. I was working," said Nicolette tactlessly, and added by way of amendment, "I was just going to bed." Which made it worse.

Having come this far, Julia decided not to be daunted. "Did you have a nice holiday?"

"Yes. Wonderful. Come in a moment." Julia followed her in, feeling almost ill with anticipation and fear. But the drawing-room was empty. She saw that Nicolette had observed her glance towards the bedroom, and sat down quickly, unable to mask a wild and desperate stare at that impassive face. "I'm very sorry—to—barge in like this. I'm afraid I don't feel very well. I—I think I drank too much at that party."

"That was naughty of you." This time there was no motherly exclamation of *pauvre petite*. "I will get you some *bicarbonate de soude*."

Julia looked round the room unhappily. Books and notes were scattered over the table in the dining alcove, under a reading lamp. Her hopes fluttered for a moment. Bernard had gone out and would be back. She got up and walked quickly over. But they were Nicolette's books. Julia glanced at the notes, inverting the weak principles of her graphology by reading what she thought she knew into the handwriting: slanted but neat, masculine and ruthless. "You are better?" Nicolette's tone sounded ironical as she came in with a small glass of white liquid.

"I still feel a little sick," Julia lied. "It's better if I stand." She swallowed the medicine with a grimace. "Thank you so much. I was just looking at your books. Did you find all you wanted in Pompeii?" She leant against the table fingering the books, uneasily playing for time. "Do tell me all about it."

"Another day, my dear. I don't want to wake him up."

Julia caught her breath. "He's asleep? Oh, I'm so sorry, I must go."

"You haven't seen him, have you? Would you like to?"

Julia stared at her. "But—I don't want to wake him."

"Oh, the light won't wake him. Only voices. At that age they sleep—*comme une trombe*.

"At—that age?"

Nicolette seemed to be enjoying the situation. "He is eleven. Lucien, my son. He goes back to school soon."

It drilled through her, downwards, unbearable, the pain spinning down from the back of her neck to the entrails, drilling, drilling deep. Bernard had a son. By another woman. And he hadn't told her. A spasm of desire and jealousy needled her emptiness. The room veered round her and ice gripped her temples again. She grabbed the table. Then the room went black.

"Juli-ah."

Nicolette's voice came from Naples at least. Julia was first aware of the leg of the table, then of a slamming pain in her head, then of Nicolette's wet handkerchief on her brow. She lay still, shutting her eyes again, knowing she would be sick if she got up now. Then she opened them and gazed silently past Nicolette's face at a crack in the ceiling, which seemed to reflect the cold crevice in her head. Slowly her blood flowed back.

"I'm sorry, I'm very sorry." She sat up and repeated it, hypnotised by the double meaning. "I'm very sorry, Nicolette, I'm very sorry."

"*Pauv' petite.* Can you walk to the sofa? You must lie down." Nicolette put her arm round her and helped her to get up. She was very tender as she supported her towards the sofa.

"You should not drink so much. It is bad, very bad. They mix all the drinks in those horrible cocktails. There, you will feel better soon. Would you like some tea? Or a *tisane*?"

"No, I'm fine, thank you."

She felt the tears scalding her eyes, and put her hand up to shade them. At last she had to ask that question.

"Where's Bernard?" Then she added quickly, "I'm glad he wasn't there to see me in a drunken state. He thinks I'm a reliable scholar." She gave a little laugh that sounded more like a choke.

"He stayed in Paris to work on an Anglo-Norman manuscript. He'll be back in a few days." She spoke quietly, and stroked Julia's hair. "Don't worry. I shall not tell him you were drunk."

Julia wondered what she would tell him.

"He admires you very much. You must go on with this book, you know."

Nicolette was playing a very strange game. Did she want to throw them together again? Or did she suppose an innocent relationship would be re-established? Or had she believed it to be innocent all the time? 'Perhaps,' thought Julia, 'she thinks I'm pregnant. Or she's pitying me. Or being ironical.' She decided to take up the cue. On she went about her doubts, her academic uncertainty, repeating and elaborating the conversation she had had with Marion. Anything to allay Nicolette's suspicions, to gain her sympathy for worries that were now only half real. And she had enough surplus emotion to re-enact them, very convincingly. Nicolette was more than polite: she wore a new, understanding face, and let her talk on in spite of the threat to her son's anglo-norman sleep.

"Forgive me, Nicolette—for keeping you up so late."

"It is nothing. You must not take things so seriously."

"No."

"You're tired. Did you not have a holiday?"

"No." She remembered too late her previous lie about going away in July, and added quickly, "I must go." It sounded rather abrupt. "Could I see—your little boy?"

"But of course."

She had never noticed the small room where Lucien now slept. His hair was darker than Bernard's, and straighter.

"He looks very pale," she whispered.

Nicolette shut the door. "He is less pale than he was, after Italy. He works hard at the *Lycée*."

"I see."

On her way out she saw something else she had never noticed, or which had not been there before: a small picture of the *Madonna del Divino Amore* from Rome, tucked behind the hall mirror. "You are Catholic?"

"Of course."

They looked at each other in silence.

"Forgive me," she said again, "for imposing on you."

Julia went home by taxi. For the first time in months, she prayed by her bed.

## Chapter Twenty-Three

"WE never launch our authors," Mr Tweedie's biggest rival publisher would say to him, "and we never give parties for them. But we love them."

Mr Tweedie would smile a shrewd Scots smile and reply: "Aye, that's a point of view. But we find it pays to make them love themselves. There's nothing like an ah'th'rr's boosted ego to produce guid average-selling stuff."

But Mr Gottlieb would shake his head. "Yes, and look what happens to the firms who spend vast sums on entertainment and splashed advertising. They're all bought up by Gottlieb's."

"Och, away wi' ye, man. Ye'll never buy up Tweedie's."

Mr Tweedie knew very well that Gottlieb's huge turnover turned partly on a regular output of bestsellers and largely on money invested in breweries. Their average sellers and their non-selling prestige authors were treated most casually. They were a duty: the former to keep the market in *perpetuum mobile*, the latter to uphold the firm's brow high and to maintain its name among the more cultural periodicals. And if a writer of whom much had been expected got rave reviews in these periodicals but turned out to sell badly, he could hardly expect individual attention. He should, on the other hand, be grateful, personally, to the great, avuncular Mr Gottlieb for printing him at all. "I am well aware," Mr Gottlieb would say, "that today's prestige sellers are often tomorrow's bestsellers." And he was convinced that he himself had brought about any such lucky transitions in his firm, all on his own. Until that change occurred, however, he took little interest in his non-sellers.

Mr Tweedie believed in flattering his authors, all his authors. He would advertise them widely, although it had long been proved that advertisements rarely sold a book but did please the author: they made him feel important, so that he would write another, and probably a better book, fairly quickly. Mr Tweedie gave parties, to which he invited other authors, other publishers, agents, reviewers, and the right sprinkling of impressionable laymen and women who would goggle suitably, gush, fawn, and buy his authors' books. Moreover, parties not only made the writer feel wanted, they also brought him into contact with all the temptations of literary life, the agents, the rival publishers, the uncajolable reviewers. 'If he survived that test,' thought Mr Tweedie, 'he was all right. He might actually get on well with his publisher.' The result of this policy meant that Tweedie and Tweedie rarely produced a bestseller. But all their average authors sold steadily. And this gave Mr Tweedie much leeway for his more experimental interests, namely, as Justin had said, highbrow pornography obscure enough to escape the comprehension of the indignant public and the experts in obscene libel; complex fantasies in symbolism translated from various foreign tongues; and now, a scholarly list. Bernard's book *Courtly Love* was just coming out. The party which Mr Tweedie gave in the last week of September was not, in fact, a launching session in Bernard's honour. Mr Tweedie never launched a book with alcohol. But Bernard was invited. Through the mosaic of heads, Julia spotted him long before he noticed her. He was brown after his holiday. Nicolette stood near him, elegant, vivacious, and self-assured. Julia was talking to Georgina, who was back from the Lake District. The weather had been drizzly there, and she looked pale, but striking in dark green taffeta shot with purple, so that her long red hair suggested a sunset over heather.

"Hussein asked me to say he sent you a dove of peace from the sea." Georgina looked startled. "A dove?"

Julia explained how the metaphor had arisen. "I read your *haiku* poems," she went on quickly, anxious not to upset her. "They were very fine."

"Thank you." Her voice was quiet. "I very nearly went back to Japan. Got as far as corresponding with the Foreign Office. But Angela Kriss bullied me into staying to take my degree next summer."

"She's right, you know."

"Of course she's right. There's never any doubt about what's right."

"The only doubt is about the wrongness of wrong," said Julia, watching Bernard, who was talking to Tweedie. Nicolette had engaged with Justin, and seemed to have forgiven him, now that Bernard's book was in hard covers with a sober dust-jacket.

"Hi, you beautiful dolls," said a tragic voice, followed by Desmond's two pairs of eyes and, much to his regret, only one pair of fondling hands. Georgina gave him the calmly freezing look that Julia had always envied, and Desmond dropped his right arm from her. It was not a priggish look, nor a dignified look, nor a solemn look, nor was it disgusted, offended, or angry. It merely said, in a friendly way: "Touching is part of making love; there is the right place for that, and the right man."

Julia lacked this grace. When Englishmen began to treat women almost as affectionately as they treated their pets—which only seemed to happen at parties—she felt embarrassed and was afraid of appearing a prude. Desmond's hand continued therefore to use the small of her back as base, from which it made frequent reconnaissance expeditions in all directions. But Desmond was tactful with Georgina. It had somehow got around, either from Julia's evasiveness when questioned, or through the radar of literary gossip, that she was not, after all, marrying "her Negro."

All the same, this was her first appearance since the poetry reading, and he was obviously trying very gently to find out more about his guest of honour's mysterious vanishing trick. Julia left them together, knowing that lies, half-lies, or bitter truth are all easier when unwitnessed. She made her way towards Justin and Nicolette, perhaps as a half-way house to Bernard.

"Juli-ah. How are you? I hope you are not drinking too much?" She turned to Justin. "Juli-ah came to my flat completely drunk the other night, and fainted."

Julia looked annoyed and Justin, who disliked Nicolette, said reproachfully, "you mustn't tell tales out of school." He nearly added, "*c'est méchant*", but remembered in time that his accent wasn't up to her French intolerance. "How's the book getting on?" he asked Julia, a little too amiably.

Justin understood women very well, and had a natural flair for a situation. He enjoyed putting Nicolette out of countenance by paying more attention to Julia, especially with the pretence that his professional interest in her was only a pretence.

"Not very well, I'm afraid." Julia half hoped he knew more and half felt that he didn't. "I've done three chapters, but somehow the summer"—she looked at Nicolette, who was watching her—"I don't know, it was difficult to get any work done, one way and another." She laughed. "Post-thesis reaction probably. It seems such a boring book now."

"Ah, you're showing all the correct symptoms," said Justin knowledgeably. "This is nothing. Ring me up just after you've passed the half-way mark, you'll need a real ego-building lunch by then."

"You did not give Berr-narr such encouragement." Nicolette laughed in a slightly forced manner. "Men are all the same."

"Oh, but I did." Justin was enjoying the success of his little act. "Bernard and I almost wrote that book together. He sat on my lap every afternoon and I guided his hand."

Julia laughed. "I don't suppose I'll get as far as half-way. What with taking up a job next month. I doubt whether I'll be able to stick to the schedule of the contract."

"Of course you will. We'll ask for the advance to be paid back if you don't, that'll make you work." He smiled at her and said in a loud stage whisper, "I'll tell you a professional secret: all authors are bone lazy. They seize on any excuse not to write. They hate writing, and they have to be whipped."

"What's all this delicious fetishism?" Desmond's four eyes peered round Julia' shoulder, leering and suggestive. "Hi, Justin."

"Hello." An imperceptible recognition of one-time familiarity flickered between them. "My dear Desmond, you are going to get our new book reviewed, aren't you? Bernard Reeves' *Courtly Love*."

"Just-in!"

"I'm so sorry, this is Mrs Reeves, Desmond Sykes." He knew very well that her reproach was not for the delayed introduction.

"How do you do," said Desmond, eyeing her expertly. "Well, of course, there's only one person to do that. Our sexy young mediaevalist here." He put his arm round Julia, promenading it up and down. Julia's glance shot across the room at Bernard, who was still with Tweedie. Then she caught Nicolette's eye. She removed Desmond's arm and said nothing.

"Just-in. Take this horrible man away. I want to talk to Juli-ah. Go away."

Desmond raised his eyebrows lecherously at Justin, who laughed and took him off, deserting him almost at once for Georgina. He wanted to talk about Hussein.

"It is all wrong, "said Nicolette. "Books should not be reviewed by friends of the author."

Julia was annoyed. "A reviewer who knows the author, intimately"—she was reckless—"is likely to be more severe rather than less."

"Precisely." Nicolette quickly turned her objection upside down, ignoring the beginning of Julia's sentence.

The conversation was difficult. Nicolette, who had been so kind in her moment of strength, seemed nervous and irritable. Had Bernard perhaps quietened her suspicions when *en famille* in Italy, then veered round again since his return? Had they quarrelled? Had she perhaps not known after all, and learnt since? Had Bernard confessed all? Julia's imagination was in a whirl. In the middle of sentence, she caught Bernard's eye at last. He stared incredulously for a second then looked away. But after a while he disentangled himself from his publisher, whom he had lobbied until then as authors of first books are apt to do, and moved round the room towards Justin and Georgina. Perhaps this too was by way of being a halfway house. She couldn't help following him round the room with her eyes, and saw that Justin was watching her over Georgina's shoulder. In spite of herself, her gaze implored his help. He narrowed his eyes and inclined his head very slightly. As soon as he could he brought them over.

"Georgina wants to talk to you," said Justin, and tactfully re-engaged Nicolette, together with Bernard, talking about his book. The rest, he thought, was up to Bernard. Nicolette started taxing him about pushing for reviews.

"What's all this about?" Georgina asked. "I haven't anything special to say."

"Oh, nothing." Julia edged her away. "A little manoeuvre of Justin's to save me from Nicolette. He saw I was in difficulties."

"Who's Nicolette?"

"Bernard Reeves' wife."

"I see."

"She's nice really." Julia tried to sound casual. "Just being tiresome about me reviewing her husband's book."

Georgina was looking at her with great sympathy. "D'you mind if we sit down?"

"No, of course not." They made their way to a group of leather armchairs no-one was using. Georgina flopped down, looking worn out.

"I say, you feeling all right?"

"Yes, fine. Just wanted to take the weight of my feet. Shoes hurting." Then she added suddenly, "perhaps I do want to talk to you." Her voice dropped. "I'm going to have a child."

Julia stared. She noticed for the first time that Georgina was drinking tomato-juice. "What are you going to do?"

"Have a child, of course."

"But—what about your degree?"

"I shall take it. Afterwards. The baby's due in April."

"You must be mad." Envy stabbed at her, not only for the child but for Georgina's poise.

"No. I'll manage."

"I think you will, too." She looked at her in admiration, aware of the enormous problems Georgina would be facing.

"I want the child," Georgina said simply, and added with a smile, echoing Hussein's manner, "a single stick smokes but does not burn."

"Tell me. Does Hussein know?"

Georgina shook her head. "You must promise me not to write to him. He would only come back. And it wouldn't work." She put her hand on Julia's. "You promise?" Julia nodded. "I wanted you to know because I thought, somehow—it might—perhaps—help you."

Julia was silent.

At this moment Bernard joined them. "Hello, Julia. I hear you're going to review my book."

Julia suddenly felt very cold. He sat down on the arm of the chair, nodding at Georgina. "I don't know," Julia said, looking at her shoes and wishing her voice would keep steady. "It's not fixed yet, and Nicolette seems to be against it."

"Oh, she's just in a mood."

Georgina got up. "Of course she must review it. I'll go and talk to Desmond at once."

"Bless you, Georgina," said Julia, with at least three different levels of meaning in her tone.

Bernard sat down in the vacated armchair and leant forward, twiddling his glass in both hands. She started twirling her hair nervously. "Hello," he said very softly.

"Hello."

"I've missed you. My God, I've missed you."

Julia looked at him with troubled eyes. She felt like saying "how like a man", but that reminded her of Desmond. Out of a hundred things she could have said, from "well, I didn't" or "why didn't you call?" to "I've missed you too", she could only quip bitterly, "I thought men could switch it off like a light."

"Superficially, yes." He leant further forward, almost touching her knee, "you can't generalise like that. Some loves are superficial for either sex." He paused and looked at her carefully. "I had to keep away. A change of gear in any relationship is painful business."

She said nothing. Once again, she was astonished at his apparent confidence. It was almost like their first meeting, except that he knew her better. Like Paul, he had come to miss her later, but unlike Paul, he was weak in the realisation of love her presence caused. He had been strong enough at the Congress, when, in his self-absorption, he felt he could do without her. Now he was, in effect, proposing what she herself had wanted. She knew in a flash that there was nothing so tender in life, not even the height and folly of passion, as the love, so rarely achieved, between ex-lovers: the deeper understanding, the stimulation of desire still there but dormant, the need without the torment. She only wondered whether the break she had asked for, and so unfortunately got, had been long enough, whether the desire was, in fact, dormant. And she knew, from the way he looked at her, that his was not.

"I don't know what you want, Bernard," she said slowly, "but please, don't play with me."

"I'm not playing with you." His knees were touching hers. "We both went round the bend for a bit. It was unwise. But there's no reason why we shouldn't keep it light-hearted. We were so happy." His voice was very low. They were shielded by standing groups, all engrossed in loud literary conversation.

"Bernard, it's over. Don't pretend there's something left when there isn't."

He touched her hand and murmured, "there is for me."

In that sense, there was for her, too, and he knew it. She shook her head. "We may still want each other," she said, staring into her glass, not daring to look at him, "but between your feelings and my feelings, that ineffable something which makes a relationship possible has been slowly strangled by your colossal self-absorption. I tried to meet it with my own selfishness, and I tried to meet it with complete selflessness. But one can't meet selfishness, one can only contain it. I wouldn't know how."

"What do you want?" he asked. "What did you expect?"

"Nothing very big. The little things. Paul gave me the spirit, the humour and the poetry of life. Like Hussein and Georgina. You cured me of one obsession by giving me another. But I still love Paul."

"Do you see him?"

She shook her head. "He's left for Sanuri."

He looked at her with a new compassion, far removed from the unaltruistic sympathy which had first brought him to her doorstep. "I know I'm selfish." He was suddenly very humble and his eyes filled with a trouble look.

"So am I. Oh, darling, this isn't a reproach, it's a statement of incapacity. I haven't enough emotion left for a recriminating scene, I assure you." Nevertheless, she felt impelled to carry out the post-mortem. She spoke very low and fast, the crystallised accumulation of thoughts melting in the warmth of his presence, pouring out calmly, smoothly, like a small spring stream. "We're so alike, yet our two kinds of selfishness are mutually exclusive. You shield yourself behind yours. I express myself through mine, yes, even at my most generous. I couldn't reach you, Bernard, you left me nothing to love but your body, and that's not what I really want."

"Isn't it? Darling."

"No. Not this way."

"Yet we gave each other—something. Oh, darling, what happened to us?"

"I don't know."

"We're collaborators on a book, you know. We might as well remain friends."

"Collaborators in Adultery."

"On paper."

She felt very sad. Julia, in fact, didn't know what she wanted. "Why didn't you tell me you had a son?" A waiter bent down with a large tray full of glasses. Julia shook her head, afraid of getting maudlin.

"I honestly don't know." He spoke quietly. The waiter moved off. "I think, perhaps, out of fear, of myself. At first it seemed irrelevant. Then I felt I could produce the fact, simply as a fact, if the subject of leaving Nicolette cropped up." She stared at him. "To myself, I mean," he added gently. "And it did, several times."

"Why do you still lie to me, Bernard?"

"I'm not lying."

"Nicolette is a Catholic. She wouldn't divorce you."

"I said leaving, not divorcing."

"I see."

"And on another level,"—he went on with his explanation—"though it may sound callous, I often seem to forget I have a son. Eleven years is a long time, you know. He's in France most of the year, at the *Lycée*. He lives with his grandparents and we go and see him in the summer. We took him to Italy this time."

"But isn't that rather strange?"

"It has certainly estranged him from me. Perhaps that's what Nicolette tried to do, I don't know. He's just a smart little French boy."

Then Julia knew what she had wanted: to be married to Paul, *non consummatus* as the Church would advise, and to have Bernard's children, lots of them. She turned her head away, overcome with shame.

"Whoever's that?" said Justin's voice just above her. He had moved up again with Desmond. Georgina seemed to have vanished. Nicolette was talking to Mr Tweedie. Julia followed his gaze and saw Professor Jarvis-Andersen, blond and bulky, followed by Marion.

"Ah," said Desmond gloomily, "the mother of all father-complexes. His wife is the novelist, Marion Farquharson."

Bernard rose to greet the professor, and Julia did the same, feeling confused and weary. "Good evening, sir. You remember our candidate, Miss Grampion?"

"But we have met since then: she is going to work with me." The shaggy bear smiled shyly, with a nervous forward shrug of his shoulder.

"Of course. How stupid of me." Bernard looked happy at the reminder of Julia's future presence in academic life.

"Hello, Marion," said Julia. "What are you doing at a rival publisher's party?"

"Jock Tweedie and I are old friends. Ever since Gottlieb's bought me out: my sales dropped almost at once."

It was astonishing the peace that always came over Julia in the presence of this woman. Love, literature, and learning all fell into perspective. From that moment the part became fun. She met a literary agent, a reviewer, a critic, speaking their language without feeling like an alien. "My dear chap, I had to stage a huge reconciliation with her, to get another ten thousand words of copy," she heard one author tell another.

She hovered as a mid-European exile writer talked to a French publisher, saying that English old maids are so much sprightlier than French ones because they have nearly always had at least some love-life. "*Les sheunes filles anklaises,*" he pontificated in his atrocious accent, "*sont si faciles à sétuire, après tout.*"

"*Par les étrangers,*" the Frenchman corrected him knowledgeably. "*Ce qui ne m'étonn du reste pas. Leurs hommes les traitent comme des animaux. Un moment c'est l'sentimentalité absurde et le romanticisme extravagant, un autre c'est l'indifférence et l'égoisme complet. Ça prend trop de temps, l'amour, trop d'effort. N'est-ce pas, Mademoiselle?*" The Frenchman had just seen her.

Julia smiled and nodded.

"*Pourtant,*" the mid-European put in, "*leur attitute est bien tifférente avec les femme étranshères. La passion, les émotions, le grang sérieux, tout est permis parce que c'es eksotique. N'est-ce pas, Matemoiselle?*"

"*C'est vray. C'est sollemeng quand nous avons l'owdace d'aytre féminines aussi qu'il nous traytent*—like doormats." She laughed and moved away. She didn't care. She talked to Georgina again and knew that Georgina, too, would be all right. She talked to the Honourable Mrs Robin Trout, wanting nothing out of her. Justin asked her again to review Bernard's book. She discussed the Symposium on adultery with Bernard and realised that in his own clumsy way, he had come to love her. But there would be no more pain. She remembered her zodiac and smiled: *In September the tone changes suddenly.* For the first time, Julia understood and felt Paul's selfless love. As she talked to Bernard, jostled by strangers, gazing in a trance at the floating faces and the bright lights, she knew with a quiet certainty what it really meant to annihilate self-love in order to grow into a greater love. Paul and Hussein and Georgina had all achieved this, not to the outside world, but within themselves. She tried to tell Bernard something of what she felt.

"I know," he said humbly. "We each of us need someone much more selfless than ourselves. I shall probably not find such a person. You may."

"No." She puffed thoughtfully at a cigarette for a moment. "I shall not marry." They looked at each other tenderly, then her eyelids dropped and she examined the ash of her cigarette with sudden absorption. "I'm going to become a Catholic," she added, as if she had found the answer in the smouldering paper.

"You may fall in love."

"Yes. I may fall in love." She looked up again, and straight into his eyes, unflinchingly. "I did fall in love. I am in love. But I have learnt something about myself, and about others. I've learnt that no man can give me all I want. It needs imagination to run a relationship, any relationship. And self-absorption excludes imagination, because it imposes its own values, unconsciously, on everything and everyone." She spoke gently, and smiled at him with great affection. "You're content to live uneasily with someone whose mind works quite differently, because that kind of unease is still easier than making the imaginative effort, constantly and continually, to live within her and let her live within you." Julia loved him more at that moment than at any other time, but there was no resentment, no jealousy, and suddenly, no desire. She felt inspired by drink and by released emotion, and above all by the happiness of being in contact with him at last. He was listening to her intently, without repelling in advance what she wanted to say. "A self-absorbed person can only know how he himself would react if he were another person, he can't feel what that person, being that person, actually does feel. That's why, probably, selfish people can't be truly creative, either in art or in living. They can only be interpreters, making their mistakes and scoring their successes as pianists, actors, minor artists, journalists, critics, scholars. We're both interpreters, Bernard."

"Ah, Miss Grampion," Professor Jarvis-Andersen broke in with shaggy benevolence, "can you come and see me at my college soon? We must discuss the year's programme in detail."

"Certainly, sir."

He smiled at her masculine correctness. "I want you to take the specialists next term: there are three of them doing the Language Paper. Third Year students."

"Oh, yes?" She felt astonishingly self-assured.

"Very much your own corner, I'm glad to say: Dan Michel's *The Prick of Conscience*. The problem of diphthongisation in fourteenth century Kentish."

The bare bones of language. Bernard's blue eyes met hers, amused, affectionate. There was no examination table between them now. And no misunderstanding. Julia had learnt the languages of love.

www.ingramcontent.com/pod-product-compliance
Ingram Content Group UK Ltd.
Pitfield, Milton Keynes, MK11 3LW, UK
UKHW041414180426
11947UKWH00007B/134